Shoma Narayanan took up writing as a hobby (after successively trying her hand at baking, sewing, knitting, crochet and patchwork), and was amazed at how much she enjoyed it. She is the author of the first Indian Mills and Boon novel to be released globally, and is also the author of *It's Complex!*

Shoma Narayanan

Published by
Rupa Publications India Pvt. Ltd 2017
7/16, Ansari Road, Daryaganj
New Delhi 110002

Sales Centres:

Allahabad Bengaluru Chennai
Hyderabad Jaipur Kathmandu
Kolkata Mumbai

Copyright © Shoma Narayanan 2017

This is a work of fiction. Names, characters, places and incidents are either
the product of the author's imagination or are used fictitiously
and any resemblance to any actual person, living or dead,
events or locales is entirely coincidental.

All rights reserved.
No part of this publication may be reproduced, transmitted,
or stored in a retrieval system, in any form or by any means,
electronic, mechanical, photocopying, recording or otherwise,
without the prior permission of the publisher.

ISBN: 978-81-291-XXXX-X

First impression 2017

10 9 8 7 6 5 4 3 2 1

The moral right of the author has been asserted.

Printed by

This book is sold subject to the condition that it shall not,
by way of trade or otherwise, be lent, resold, hired out, or otherwise
circulated, without the publisher's prior consent, in any form of binding or
cover other than that in which it is published.

To my amazing family
Badri, Aditya and Anousha

Prologue
....

'I'm sorry, I can't do this.'

The priest stopped mid-mantra and looked up in surprise. He had been presiding over Arya Samaj weddings for the last thirty years, and this was the first time something like this had happened. 'I don't understand,' he started to say, but the bride was already undoing the knot between her pallu and the groom's angavastra with determined, if slightly unsteady, fingers. She was an unusually pretty girl, the priest noted—he hadn't really looked at her properly until she started behaving in this completely uncharacteristic fashion.

'Damn this thing,' she muttered, and gave the fabric a final yank—the knot came apart with a rending sound.

'Zina...' the groom said, and the priest's eyes swivelled to him. The groom was tall and had an impressive physique, but his face was ugly, the priest thought. Thick black eyebrows, deep-set eyes, a hawk nose and a lantern jaw made him look like a gangster who'd moved up in life a little. For a few seconds, the priest's imagination ran wild. Perhaps the bride was being forced into this wedding—now that he thought about it, she had looked pale and unhappy when he first saw her...or hang on, that wasn't this couple, that was... The priest's wandering thoughts were jerked back into the present by a muffled gasp from the bride. The groom was now gripping her shoulders with his large hands. 'You can't do this,' he was saying urgently, as he almost shook the girl. The priest's first instinct was to demand that he unhand her, but the man's bulk made him hesitate. After all, he didn't know the groom's side of the story—it would be far better if someone from the family intervened.

Zina didn't seem intimidated in the least. 'Yes, that's exactly what I'm saying,' she said, shrugging the man's hands off her shoulders as easily as she'd have brushed away a fly.

'I can't do this. I can't marry you. I'm so sorry, Shiven. Have a happy life.' She leaned over, kissed him on the cheek and then picked up the skirt of her heavy ghaghra and ran out of the marriage hall.

For a second, the priest thought that Shiven would start after her, but his massive shoulders were already sagging in defeat. The priest sneaked a quick look at him and noted in horror that the man's eyes were filling with tears.

'Sit down, beta. This is so unfortunate...wait, let me get you some water...nothing like this has ever happened before...' He knew that he was wittering on, but he couldn't seem to stop talking. He looked helplessly towards the small family gathering that was attending the wedding, but everyone was frozen in shock. Shiven was sitting by the side of the fire now, his head in his hands, and no one seemed to know what to do. An elderly couple, probably his parents, finally got up and the woman came to Shiven. No one had gone after Zina and the priest couldn't help feeling that it was all very odd.

'Will she be all right?' he asked, leaving Shiven to the elderly couple and walking over to another couple who he assumed were the bride's parents. 'She'll be fine,' the woman hissed. 'Selfish bitch, letting him down like this. I told my nephew he shouldn't get friendly with a girl like that hairdresser or model or whatever she is!'

'Perhaps it's for the best,' her husband said consolingly. 'He'll get over this and then we can find a good girl for him from our own community.'

The priest looked around. The wedding was a small one and there were only six or seven guests, all of whom were now crowding around Shiven. 'Is there no one from the bride's family here?' he asked plaintively.

Shiven's aunt turned around to glare at him. 'No,' she snapped. 'I don't think she even had a real family. The number of lies she told us...'

'She wasn't a liar,' Shiven said flatly, getting to his feet. 'I won't hear a word against her.' His aunt began to splutter at him, but he shook his head firmly. 'Zina has every right to change her mind.'

'After half the pheras were over?' the aunt asked incredulously. 'Well, all I can say is that you're such an idiot, you deserve to be dumped in public like this!' She swung around to glare at the rest of the relatives. 'I don't know about you people, but I'm leaving now.' She glared at the priest. 'And you can stop staring—this isn't the circus, you know!'

She flounced out, followed by everyone except Shiven and his parents while the priest was still gasping in reaction to the unprovoked attack.

'I'm so sorry,' Shiven's father said to the priest. He was an older, greyer version of Shiven and he looked almost as upset as his son. 'We'll pay your full fees, of course, maybe even something more, given the...the unpleasantness. I must apologise for my sister—she was against this marriage from the beginning. But Shiven was terribly in love, and the girl seemed really nice....we never expected...'

'Will she be all right?' the priest asked again. He was almost sixty years old, but deep down he was a romantic—something about the expression on Zina's beautiful face as she fled from the wedding had touched a chord in his youthful heart.

Shiven sighed. 'She'll be all right,' he said. 'She knows how to take care of herself.'

If Zina could have heard him, she would have whole-heartedly agreed. She had spent most of her life taking care of herself—she was the eldest of four siblings and her parents had pretty much left her to bring herself up. All their care and attention had been lavished on her younger brother, and when she had announced at the ripe old age of twenty-two that she was moving to Mumbai to become a hair stylist, they'd seemed more relieved than upset. The stylist story had been a cover-up—what Zina really wanted to do, was modelling and for the first three years she'd done reasonably well; a few magazine shoots and even a TV ad. Then, inexplicably, the assignments stopped coming in and she had to go back to hairdressing.

Shiven was a customer who had fallen for her—he was a criminal lawyer and was loaded. In spite of his profession, he had fallen in love with her at first sight. It had taken several months for her to even take him seriously, and many more before she agreed to marry him. She'd not been in love with him in the least, and in hindsight, she wondered what she'd been thinking. Of course she was lonely, and he had proposed after she had a particularly bad day at work. The thought of having someone to look after her was seductive in its appeal.

'Bandra,' she told the autowallah crisply. She'd have preferred a taxi but there wasn't one in sight. The heavy zardozi embroidery on her ghaghra was weighing her down and she didn't think she could walk long enough to find a taxi. Besides, Shiven might follow her—the quicker she got away the better.

She sank into the seat with a sigh as the auto driver

jerked up a lever on the floor of the auto to start. Lucky that she'd remembered to pick up her bejewelled purse before she ran out, she thought grimly. Her worldly goods—all two suitcases of them—had been packed to be transported to Shiven's flat and she had also given up her room as a paying guest in Mrs Anthony's little flat near Almeida Park. Her suitcases were still there though, and it made sense to pick them up before Shiven tracked her down.

Digging into her bag for her phone, she typed out a Facebook update: 'Couldn't do it—still single.' Then she added a few exclamation marks for emphasis and clicked on 'Post'. Next, she changed her relationship status to 'Single'. Okay, so that was informing the world done with. Now all that remained was to figure out what she wanted to do with the rest of her life.

Mrs Anthony greeted her return with dismay. 'You didn't get married!' she exclaimed, her piggy eyes almost reaching normal size in horror. 'Oh that poor, poor boy.' She paused for a bit and said, 'I'm sorry about your room though, Zina. I just rented it out to a really sweet girl. Works in a bank, you know...'

'...and will pay her rent on time,' Zina completed for Mrs Anthony. 'And won't come home at odd hours. It's okay, Mrs A, I understand. I just need to change and pick up my suitcases, and I'll be off.'

But off where, was the real question. She couldn't afford a hotel, not a decent one at least, and most of her friends lived in shared flats or were paying guests like her.

No one had a room to spare. Running through the list again in her head, she stopped at one name. It wasn't a perfect solution, but it would have to do.

one
....

THE THING ABOUT Indore was that it was an in-between city. Big enough to have malls and traffic lights, a university and even a couple of decent hotels, but not big enough for people to mind their own business. Anjali frowned at the anonymous letter in front of her before turning it over Sherlock Holmes style, to see if there was any clue that would help her identify the sender. Predictably, there was nothing. Lucky old Sherlock had been around at a time when people wrote anonymous letters on typewriters with a few extra-worn keys and on paper that was sold only in one shop in London. Nowadays, the poison-pen types had access to laser printers and reams of industrially-produced A4, and there was no way in hell she would be able to trace the writer.

'You are married lady with child,' the letter started off, the writer clearly being more focused on technical accuracy than grammar. 'Conducting affair openly with

Prof. Khatri is shameful and bad example to innocent students. Please mend ways or we will need to inform Dr Sharma, your most respected father. Prof. Khatri is immoral man not believing in the divine God and only ruination of reputation and good name is in front of you.'

'Innocent students, my little left toe!' Anjali muttered, tearing the sheet of paper across a few times and throwing it into the wastepaper bin under her desk. A few seconds later, she leaned down to retrieve the pieces of paper from the bin. Perhaps she was being paranoid, but she wouldn't put it past one of her nosey colleagues to go through her trash. She shared a room with another woman professor who was a) not the trash-bin-scavenger type and b) was anyway on a long leave. Other people walked in and out at will.

'Tore something up by mistake?' a friendly voice asked, and Anjali looked up to see Prof. Deven Khatri, the alleged adulterer, atheist and immoral corrupter of innocent students standing at the door. He was tall and scholarly-looking and if not exactly handsome, still a pretty decent specimen of manhood. Anjali gazed at him speculatively. If it hadn't been for the annoying moustache he cultivated and the fact that she was still not over her estranged husband, she could have actually been tempted by him.

Silently, she pieced the sheet back together and pushed it towards Deven. His brows puckered up as he went through the letter and then he gave a snort of laughter.

'If only they knew,' he said ruefully. Then he caught sight of her expression. 'Is this bothering you?'

'A little. Okay, quite a lot, actually. It isn't the first letter I've had.'

Deven hesitated a little, 'Were they all...'

'...suggesting that I was having a rip-roaring affair with you? Yes.' She kept her voice low, mindful of the sharp-eared students passing by the open door. 'Actually, Deven, maybe you shouldn't drop by so often. I'm not trying to be rude, but it's giving people the wrong idea. What's the point?'

The rueful expression deepened and he stood up. 'I get it,' he said. 'I'll call you at night, is that okay?'

'I guess,' Anjali said grumpily. Deven had proposed marriage on at least three previous occasions, ignoring the minor fact that she had a husband who was still alive and kicking.

'I'll see you around then,' he said, and Anjali nodded without looking up. She had ten minutes before her next lecture, and she stuffed the pieces of paper into her purse while she pulled out her class notes to brush up.

Deven ran an impatient hand through his hair as he walked away. Anjali might be married and have a twelve-year-old kid, but she was still maddeningly attractive with her lovely Madonna face and full, curvy figure. That husband of hers was a fool, he thought savagely. To leave his young wife and daughter to go off to work in another country! No wonder their marriage was on the rocks. He'd have liked nothing better than to marry Anjali himself and settle down to happy domesticity with her, but she seemed constitutionally incapable of seeing his point of view.

Anjali was still a little perturbed when she stepped into her next class. As usual, the class was almost full—the college didn't insist on more than fifty per cent attendance in each subject, but very few students missed Prof. Anjali Dubey's lectures. Deven scowled as he passed her class a while later. His own classes were usually full as well, but that was because he inspired a very healthy respect among his students. Also, of course, because he dropped their grades for every class they bunked. Anjali's classes were full because the girls openly admired her and copied her hairstyles, while the boys developed a sudden keen interest in Chemistry after having virtually ignored the subject all through their school years. Deven's scowl worsened as he noticed a pimply young man in the last bench carefully drawing a sketch of Anjali in his notebook. It was a flattering, if somewhat disproportionate, representation especially in the chest area, and Deven had to repress a strong urge to lean in through an open window and smash the young Rembrandt's head into his wooden desk.

In time-honoured teacher tradition, Anjali had decided to give herself a little break by giving the class a surprise quiz. After she had written the questions on the board, she sat at her desk and allowed her mind to wander. She didn't even notice Deven walk past the class. The letter had bothered her even more than she had admitted to

Deven. Not for the first time, she wished that her domestic circumstances were a little more conventional. A husband would have been a convenient prop to have around—ever since she and Sushil had separated, she had had people acting weird with her. The graffiti in the college men's room featured her name many times over—coupled with a male colleague's in a few places and in others, just reflecting someone's sick fantasies. Thankfully no one had linked her with a student yet, but it was probably only a matter of time. It didn't help that most of her female colleagues were disapproving matrons in their fifties who found Anjali's bright-coloured churidar kurtas and tumbling curls an affront to their collective dignity.

'Concentrate, Aarav,' she told a student who was wriggling uncomfortably in his seat. The boys around him were grinning and nudging each other, and she frowned. She was pretty big on discipline; you had to be if you wanted to survive more than a day as a teacher in the Shantidurga College of Science and Commerce.

'Sorry Ma'am,' Aarav said, turning an agonized face up to her. He was a curly-haired, rather impish-looking kid, one of the youngest in the class. Usually, he had a bright grin plastered all over his face but today, he was contorting his face as if he was being tortured by the police.

'Are you not well?' Anjali asked, but before she could complete the question, Aarav had leapt to his feet, both hands clutching his rather childishly rounded backside. 'Owww, sorry, ouch,' was all he said, almost dancing next to his desk as he scrambled to get something out of his back pocket. 'Owww,' he said finally as he got a little bit of paper and something that looked like a little grey pebble out of his pocket and threw it in the aisle, twisting his body into weird contortions as his classmates dissolved into laughter.

Anjali sighed as soon as she saw the pebble. There was a student who tried this every year in spite of all the dire warnings issued by the Chemistry lab.

'Sodium,' she said as Aarav continued to clutch at his burnt bum. Going by his evident embarrassment, his trousers probably had a hole in them. 'Aarav, do you have your Chemistry textbook with you?'

Aarav nodded nervously.

'Great,' she said smiling pleasantly at the students, most of whom had stopped giggling and were trying to gauge her mood.

'Can someone tell me a few of the properties of sodium please?'

'Atomic number 11,' a bespectacled girl volunteered from the front row. 'Soft metal, good conductor.' She shot Aarav a quick glance. 'And umm, highly reactive, Ma'am.'

'So someone who decides to flick some from the lab and put it in his pocket would have to be pretty dumb, right?' Aarav's face fell immediately. 'I'm sorry, Ma'am,' he said. 'I thought I'd take it home and see what happened when I put it in water. The book says it'll explode, but it didn't look that dangerous. I'm really sorry, Ma'am...'

'No, I'm sorry,' Anjali said. 'For you, because I'm now going to ask you to pick up that piece of sodium and take it back very carefully to the Chemistry lab, and apologise to the lab assistant for stealing it. I need to see a note from him confirming that you've put the stuff back and it's now safely stored. Don't come back without the note. Unfortunately you'll miss the rest of the test and from what I can see, you've got two of the three questions you've attempted, wrong.' The test counted towards their year-end grades, and it was a very subdued Aarav who carefully collected the piece of sodium and carried it off.

'The rest of the class gets ten minutes extra on the test,' she announced once he was out of the door. 'And Mr Sisodia, you get minus twenty marks for cheating from Mr Tomar's answer sheet.' Having successfully defused the situation and gotten the class settled again, she went back to her desk. She had lost her chain of thought and giving up on introspection, she spent the rest of the class keeping an eagle eye on the kids so that they didn't succumb to the very natural urge to peek into their neighbours' answer sheets.

Deven called her after dinner, just after Anjali had got her daughter into bed and was ready to go to bed herself. The conversation was a difficult one, made significantly more difficult because Anjali had to hide in the garden and whisper into the phone. Finding a suitable spot was as difficult as solving a problem in differential calculus because:

a) She had to be in a place where her father and daughter couldn't hear her
b) She had to look gainfully employed if her incurably nosey neighbours peeked down from their terrace and saw her, and
c) Her phone needed to work, and there were very few spots in the garden with any signal.

She finally ended up wedged between the well and the concrete box that housed her tulsi plant, pretending to be doing stuff to the tulsi's roots. The parapet of the well was cold and clammy behind her and she had to squat ungracefully to avoid getting green algae on her knees. Luckily, it wasn't dark—her father insisted on keeping two bright halogen lights on all night to discourage burglars.

'But Deven, we're just friends!' she said in exasperation. 'I can't marry you. I've told you this so many times, I don't know how else I can make you understand!'

'A good kick in the pants should do the job,' a helpful male voice said an inch behind her ear. Anjali gave an undignified yelp and tumbled over, narrowly stopping her phone from falling into the well. Her heart rate had tripled and her eyes were wide with alarm as she scrambled to regain her balance; it didn't help that the cemented area around the well was hopelessly slippery.

'So sorry,' the owner of the voice said, not sounding sorry at all as he held out a sinewy hand to help her up, his eyes dancing with amusement. Anjali glared at him from the ground, ignoring the outstretched hand.

'Where'd you pop up from?' she asked ungraciously, though her heart was doing an uneven little bhangra in her chest. She had thought her husband was in Saudi Arabia, and embarrassing as it was to be found skulking in the garden and talking to a boyfriend, a little voice in her head insisted that it served Sushil right.

'Caught a flight, got here a few minutes ago,' Sushil said, hunkering down next to her. He gestured towards her phone which was emitting worried sounds. 'Do you want to tell lover-boy that you're a bit tied up right now? Maybe he could make an appointment to talk to you later.'

He didn't bother to keep his voice down and Anjali had a nasty feeling that Deven could hear every word. She made a face and picked up the phone. 'Deven, something's come up...I need to go.'

'All right,' Deven said, managing to sound dignified, wounded and possessive all at the same time. 'I do hope everything's all right.'

'Everything's fine,' Anjali said, and cut the call. Scrambling to her feet, she brushed off the green stains on her salwar. 'Sushil, *why* are you here? You should've told us you were coming. We might not have been at home, or we might have had people over...'

'Or you might be making plans to marry lusty young college professors,' Sushil said, shaking his head sorrowfully as he got to his feet in a single fluid movement. 'You do know that polyandry's illegal, right?'

'We're not together any longer,' Anjali said, hating how defensive she sounded.

'Right now, we're not,' he agreed. 'But that's exactly what I'm here to talk about.'

He had a familiar determined look on his face and Anjali said with foreboding, 'Oh no. Sushil, we don't want to get back together—remember how bad it was? Come on, let me get you something to eat, we can talk later when you're not all fired up.'

She was able to keep him off the topic till he finished dinner, and then he started again. It wasn't a totally unexpected onslaught. They had been separated for a while but had stayed in touch because of their daughter, Gayatri. For the last few months, the tone of Sushil's e-mails had become more and more nostalgic. Anjali had put it down to probable girlfriend trouble—Sushil always started missing her when a relationship went wrong. This was the first time he had proposed getting back together though, and Anjali was finding it difficult to come up with reasons for refusing.

'It wouldn't work,' she said for about the hundredth time.

Sushil sighed. It was a gusty sigh that seemed to imply that it wasn't easy dealing with someone who was being childish and unreasonable, and Anjali felt a strong desire to slap him.

'Anjali, how long are you going to live buried away in Indore? It was all right when we were kids and didn't know any better. But there's a big wide world out there...' he gestured so that Anjali could see quite how big and wide it was. After a few seconds, he lowered his arms and went on. 'And it is not just you, is it? You're subjecting Gayatri to the same narrow, hide-bound childhood that we had when she can have so much more!' Seeing Anjali's steely expression falter a little, he pressed further to his advantage. 'A better school, more facilities, the best private classes money can buy...'

'And having to cover her face every time she steps out of doors,' Anjali retorted. 'That's what the Middle East is like, however good the schools and the classes are. If that was what I wanted for my daughter, I can move to a village and have it right here in India. Save on the airfare too.'

Too late, she realised that she had played right into Sushil's hands. A broad smile spread across his handsome face, and he said slowly, 'Oh didn't I tell you? I've moved back to India.' He saw her expression change and immediately went on. 'I'm in Mumbai. Come on, Anjali, we've lived apart for so long... I know we've had issues, but we can put those behind and start again. Think about it, at least for Gayatri's sake, if not for us.'

'I'll think about it,' Anjali promised. 'Now go to bed. Dad sleeps very lightly nowadays. If he hears us talking this late, he'll get upset.'

'It'll be just like old times then,' Sushil said before he could stop himself. Anjali had always been his ideal of the perfect woman and he was more than ready to get back with her. He bent his head and brushed a light kiss across her lush lips, smiling slightly as she quivered in response, 'I've missed you,' he whispered against her mouth.

'I've missed you too,' Anjali said, using her last ounce of self-control to step back and away from him. 'A little. Now go to bed before we wake everyone up. I can't believe you landed up in the middle of the night like this without giving me any warning.'

He gave her a lopsided little grin and said, 'I couldn't wait to see you.'

'I'm suitably flattered,' she said drily. 'Goodnight!' And before he could say anything else, she turned and ran into her bedroom.

It was an easy decision on the face of it. Anjali was tired of living in Indore and being at the beck and call of her rather autocratic father, and the thought of living with Sushil again was terribly tempting. He had aged well, she thought as she lay awake staring at the ceiling later at night. When she had first met him he was seventeen, tall and lanky with a shock of unruly hair and a smile that made her insides go all squirmy. They dated clandestinely for a few years, and when they were out of college, they told their parents that they were getting married.

According to her father, their marriage was doomed to fail. 'Too young,' he grunted. 'The fellow doesn't even have a proper job.'

It had taken Sushil less than a month to land a 'proper job', and for the first few years of their marriage they'd been blissfully happy. Sure they'd had to live with Sushil's mom and she had some pretty annoying habits; expecting Anjali to wear a sari whenever she stepped outside the house was one. Having a bhajan CD on at top volume all through the day, always the same one, was another. But all in all, she was a nice enough mother-in-law and her amazing cooking skills made up for having Anup Jalota blaring into your ears all day long. Then Gayatri was born and Sushil decided that an entry-level engineering job in a fibre optics company wasn't enough for a man with a family to support. He took a job with a company in Saudi Arabia without even discussing it with Anjali properly. Or rather, they'd discussed it. Anjali had said no and that she didn't want to go there. He had gone ahead and taken the job anyway.

'Selfish and money-minded,' was what Anjali's father had said then, but she had defended Sushil hotly. 'You can go join him after the baby is a little older,' Sushil's mother had said, giving her a comfortable smile. But a few months later, Sushil's mother was dead—a sudden stroke followed by a heart attack. All those parathas and bowls of gajar halwa had led to her being hopelessly overweight and her arteries were apparently so clogged that it was a miracle she had stayed alive this long. Anjali had actually been more affected than Sushil. Her own mother had died when she was in her teens, and Mrs Dubey had been an invaluable source of strength when Gayatri was born.

Maybe that was when she should have joined Sushil,

Anjali thought, tossing restlessly in bed. Except that Sushil had no longer seemed keen about it and her father had told her that there was no way he was letting her go to Saudi Arabia. So she had moved back to the house she had grown up in, and her daughter became the focus of her life. A year later, Sushil and she had a big show-down, during which he insisted that either she moved to Saudi or they separate. She had chosen separation and since then they'd never discussed the possibility of getting back together. Perhaps it could work, she thought drowsily. They were both older now and, hopefully, wiser and she was tired of living alone. Also, she missed having a man in her life... Turning over, she snuggled into her pillow as her eyes drifted shut.

'You didn't tell me Papa was here!' Gayatri sounded more surprised than annoyed, and Anjali smiled as she looked up. Twelve years old, with long flowing hair and a piquant little face, Gayatri was the most perfect child she had ever seen. Anjali kept telling herself that she was hopelessly biased, but lots of people seemed to agree with her.

In some ways, Gayatri was like Sushil—as single-minded and driven, but the drive came tempered with a particularly sweet nature and an ability to charm the socks off the crankiest adult. Even her grandfather wasn't exempt.

Sushil stood up and pulled his daughter into his arms. Gayatri hugged him back enthusiastically. In spite of his long absences and estrangement from his wife, he was an excellent father and Gayatri adored him.

'How long are you here for?' she demanded. 'A day? A week? Did Mom tell you about the drawing competition I won?'

'A few days,' Sushil said. 'And yes, she told me, and she showed me the drawing as well. What was it supposed to be, the Abominable Snowman?'

Gayatri gave him a fake punch in the arm. 'It's a drawing of *you*!' she said. 'The theme was "My Awesome Dad". Though if you thought it was a picture of a Yeti, I don't know...maybe I should have called it "My Short-sighted Dad", or "My Really Ugly Dad-Who-Looks-Like-a-Yeti".'

'Don't be cheeky,' Anjali said automatically, but she was smiling. Evidently encouraged by the smile, Gayatri asked, 'So can I bunk school today?'

'I don't think so,' Sushil and Anjali said together. 'But Nanaji says I don't learn anything worthwhile there, and I've seen Daddy after so long... Pleeeaaase?'

Sushil looked at Anjali and she hesitated a little before making up her mind. She had to go to work herself, and it wouldn't hurt Sushil to know that he couldn't walk into their lives unannounced and expect them to drop everything.

'I think you'd better go,' she said gently. 'But tell you what, you can skip Sanskrit tuition and come home directly after school. I'll speak to Mrs Singh.'

Anjali's father came into the kitchen and frowned as he

heard the last part of the sentence. He didn't say anything though, but he gave Sushil a curt nod before sitting down at the large breakfast table.

'Poha?' Anjali asked her father nervously.

'Yes,' he said, peering at the large bowl in the centre of the table. 'Is that coconut in it?'

Gayatri came around the table and gave him an exuberant hug—she was in a wonderful mood and didn't care who knew it.

'Yep, it's coconut,' she said. 'And don't say it's bad for your heart. There's barely one gram of it in there.'

Anjali had spent her entire life in complete awe of her father and watching her daughter expertly twist him around her little finger was an ongoing revelation. He was smiling reluctantly now, as Gayatri ladled the poha onto his plate.

'I'm off to school now,' she announced. 'Don't fight when I'm away, okay people?'

'Have you done your homework?' Anjali asked. 'What about that word list?'

'I have it by heart,' Gayatri said smugly. 'Ask me something.'

'Onomatopoeia,' Anjali said promptly.

Gayatri's brow puckered up, and she spelt it out slowly but correctly.

'Good,' Anjali's father said. 'Do you know what it means?'

'Umm, something to do with the way words sound?'

'Look it up in the dictionary,' Anjali said. Gayatri made a face. 'Mom, tell me, no, please? Dad?'

'It means a person who pees on a mat,' Sushil said. 'On-a-mat-pee-er.'

Gayatri giggled but Anjali glared at Sushil. Her father grunted. It was the sort of grunt that seemed to express his opinion of Sushil's intellectual capabilities, and Anjali winced. It was probably natural for Dr Mishra to be judgemental at his age, but it certainly didn't make for easy conversation around him.

Sushil got to his feet as soon as Gayatri left. 'I think I'll go out for a bit,' he said. 'Got a few people to meet, and there's some stuff I need to sort out at the bank.' 'Aren't you leaving for college?' Dr Sharma asked half an hour later as it finally dawned on him that Anjali was still puttering around in the kitchen. She shook her head. 'I wanted to talk to you,' she said. 'Sushil's moving to Mumbai and he wants Gayatri and me to move there with him.'

For a minute, Anjali thought he hadn't heard her, and she was about to repeat the sentence when he said, 'Yes, I thought it was something like that.' He fell silent, staring into space and Anjali noticed with a slight sense of shock how tired he looked.

'You should go,' he said, and she looked at him in surprise.

'I thought you'd be against the idea!' she exclaimed. 'I'm undecided myself.'

'It's the best thing for Gayatri,' he said. 'And even for

you. You're still young, living like this with your father and daughter. It isn't good for you. I know you're very careful, but sooner or later... you're only human, after all.'

It took her a few seconds to understand what he was saying, and then her face flamed up in embarrassment. Okay, so there had been some gossip about her and Deven, but she hadn't realised it had reached her father. Or at least, nothing serious enough for her father to accuse her of being ripe for an affair, and an indiscreet one at that.

'It'll be good for Gayatri,' she said. 'But what about you? Would you want to come to Mumbai with us, or...' It had been Sushil's suggestion that they rent a flat near theirs, perhaps in the same apartment complex, for her father. Given that the two men had never got along, it was a very generous gesture and it had tilted the scales in favour of moving.

But her father was already shaking his head. 'I'll be fine on my own,' he said. 'And if I need help, Arvind is only a couple of houses down the road.'

Arvind was Anjali's brother. When he married, he moved into his own house. Privately, Anjali thought it was the only reason he was still on talking terms with his father and still married to his wife, but a lot of people felt it was odd for him to live separately.

Odd or not, Anjali felt very thankful that Arvind hadn't moved out of Indore. Her father was an old curmudgeon, but she was very fond of him, and leaving him alone with no family around would be unthinkable.

Sushil's face lit up when Anjali told him. 'Brilliant!' he said. 'When can you move?'

'I'll complete this semester's classes and we can move immediately after that,' she said. 'And we'll have to figure out a school for Gayatri, won't we?'

'We'll have to tell her first,' Sushil said. They were alone in the house—Prof. Dubey had headed off to a friend's place for a game of chess, and Sushil was standing very close to her now, so close that she could feel his breath stirring her hair.

'She'll be thrilled,' Anjali said, trying to sound as brisk and practical as she possibly could, though she was very conscious of Sushil's nearness. It had been several years since they'd last touched, and all kinds of horrid little practicalities shoved themselves into her mind. She hadn't turned the gas off, her legs weren't waxed, and while she was wearing a new kameez, her innerwear was ancient and had been chosen for strictly practical purposes. Sushil's hands were on her arms now, his fingers gently caressing the sensitive spot inside her elbow.

'Are *you* thrilled?' he murmured close to her ear, and Anjali wriggled away. 'Stop it,' she said, a little breathlessly. 'I'm in the middle of making lunch and Gayatri will be home from school any minute now.'

'We have an hour before she gets home,' Sushil said, his lazy smile crinkling up the corners of his eyes. 'Turn off the gas, and let's go to bed.'

The approach was so blunt that Anjali gaped at him

in dismay. It was almost three years since they'd last slept together, and her first reaction was to wonder if she still knew what to do. Sushil leaned across her and turned a knob to put the gas stove off. Then he bent down and kissed her swiftly, his lips comfortably familiar and wildly exciting all at the same time. His voice was a little rough when he finally lifted his head.

'Which room?' he asked, and Anjali's protests died on her lips as she looked up at him. Sushil's eyes were his most attractive feature—deep-set and fringed with short, thick eyelashes, they could focus on you to the exclusion of everyone else in the world. Right now, they had the slightly glazed look that she remembered from earlier lovemaking sessions. His hands were already wandering over her body, and the last little shreds of doubt in Anjali's mind dissolved as he began to nuzzle the nape of her neck. He might have been a crap husband in many ways, but Sushil had always been phenomenal in bed. Agreeing to give their marriage another shot and then acting coy about sex would be a bit like paying for a five-course buffet dinner and refusing to touch the dessert.

'Dad and I wanted to check something with you,' Anjali said when Gayatri got back from school. Gayatri looked up at them enquiringly. 'If it's about swimming lessons, I still want to learn,' she said.

'Well, we can talk about swimming lessons as well,' Sushil said, tweaking her plaits. 'But it was something a little more serious.'

'Swimming is serious,' she said. 'But anyway, shoot.'

'How do you feel about moving to Mumbai?' Sushil asked. 'I'm back in India now, and I've rented a place in an apartment complex that incidentally has a fabulous swimming pool.'

Gayatri stared at him. 'Move to Mumbai?' she asked, and her evident dismay made Sushil's heart clench in his chest. He should have come back to India years ago and spent more time with Gayatri when she was growing up. One regretful thought chased another through his brain, but he tried not to let any of it show as he said gently, 'Yes, you can take some time and think about it. Ask us any questions that you want...'

'But what about Mum?' Gayatri asked, her eyes darting between the two of them. 'Where will she be?'

Sushil looked surprised. 'She'd move as well, of course.' Then, as he saw a look of relief spread over her little face, he said gently, 'I wouldn't try to take you away from her, sweetheart. I want all of us to live together again, like a proper family.'

Gayatri, for the first time in her short life, appeared to be at a loss for words, and Anjali stepped in. 'You loved Mumbai when we went there for a holiday, didn't you? I'm sure you'll like living there.'

She nodded, but she was clearly torn. She had dreamed of her parents getting back together, but she hadn't expected it to really happen, and definitely not all of a sudden like this. When she imagined it, she had always thought Sushil would come back to Indore.

'What about my friends?' she asked suddenly. 'And Nanaji? Will he come with us?' In spite of being as tall as Anjali, she looked suddenly so lost and child-like that Anjali put her arms around her as she began explaining why Gayatri's grandfather wasn't coming along.

It was probably the thought that she could still come back to Indore for holidays and that the house she had grown up in, would be as it always was, that made Gayatri reconcile to leaving her grandfather behind. Sushil stayed silent throughout the conversation. He didn't dislike Anjali's father, but the two men were very different and it never failed to amaze Sushil that his daughter was so close to her grandad. 'It's like watching a kitten cuddle up to a grizzly,' he muttered once Gayatri was out of the room. 'And your dad's just bad. I actually saw him smile four times today. Must be a world record.'

'Stop it,' Anjali said automatically, but her mind was far away. Now that the decision was taken, there was one person she definitely needed to tell before the news spread.

'Have you thought it through?' Deven asked her quietly when he came around to meet her a few days later. 'You weren't happy earlier. How do you know things will work this time around?'

'It's the best thing for Gayatri,' Anjali said. 'I'm sorry

Deven. I let you get the wrong idea, but the thing is, even if I wasn't going back to Sushil it would never have worked between us.'

'I realise that now,' Deven said. He was gentlemanly enough not to say that he'd have realised it a lot earlier if Anjali hadn't strung him along, but she couldn't help feeling horribly guilty all the same. It had been mainly vanity that had made her do it. Vanity and the desire to prove to herself that she could manage without Sushil—she couldn't feel proud of either emotion, and was heartily relieved when Deven finally got up to leave.

'I'll stay in touch,' Anjali promised as she saw him to the door, knowing fully well that she wouldn't. She heaved a little sigh of relief as she shut the door. Seeing Deven in her home had finally driven in the fact that she had been crazy to even consider hooking up with him. He was the kind of man her father would have chosen for her—maybe that was why her subconscious had done its best to con her into falling for him. It hadn't quite succeeded, and now that Sushil was back, she couldn't imagine herself with anyone else.

Dear Papa,

I'm so happy we're shifting to Mumbai. I'm looking forward to seeing you again. But I'll miss Nanaji and my friends, especially my best friend Ananya.

Mummy told me that your flat is in Bandra. I forgot to ask you—can you see the sea from the windows?

Love,
Gayatri

two

'I WANT TO rent the hoarding on top of your building,' Shiven said. The building secretary looked a little nonplussed—evidently, he wasn't used to people trying to rent hoardings the way they rented flats. 'I'll give you the number of our media agency,' he said. 'You can book it, but I think a bank has it for the next couple of weeks, and after that there's some travel company...'

'I'll give you double of whatever they offer,' Shiven said, and the man goggled at him. 'But Mr Patil, it doesn't work that way. We have a contract with the agency!'

Shiven dug into his pocket for a card and shoved it across the table to Mr Shah. 'I'm a lawyer,' he said simply. 'Show me the contract, and I'll find you a way to get out of it.'

If Mr Shah was dismayed by Shiven's strong-arm tactics, he was horrified by what Shiven finally put up on the hoarding.

'Zina, I love you. Come back to me,' the hoarding said in big bold letters. 'This is shameful, Mr Shah,' the other society members told him, but unlike the media agency's contract, the one they'd signed with Shiven was unbreakable. And things became worse when Zina painted a sign on a white bedsheet with red acrylic paint and hung it out of her window. Her lettering was terrible, but one could hardly miss the foot-high letters that asked the simple question 'Who are you?'

'My men will come and change the flex on the hoarding tomorrow,' Krish told Mr Shah. 'Please let your security people know.'

There was nothing Mr Shah could do to stop him, and the next day, the hoarding said 'Zina, will you marry me?' And below the letters, there was a huge blow-up of Shiven's signature.

'This is getting ridiculous,' Sushil said as he let himself into his flat two days later. Zina was huddled over yet another white bedsheet with a pot of paint. 'The least you could do is buy your own goddamn bedsheets.'

Zina shrugged. 'This one had a ketchup stain on it anyway. How was the trip? Wifey agreed to come back?'

'Yes,' Sushil said. 'She's moving to Mumbai next month. That gives you enough time to find a place for yourself.'

'Hmm,' Zina said, and picking up the sheet she crossed the room to carefully hang it out of the window. In large purple letters, it announced to the world 'In your dreams, loser!'

'Not very subtle, are you?' Sushil said drily. 'Why don't you guys just talk on the phone?'

'How simple, why didn't I think of that?' Zina said, wandering across the room to pick up a manicure kit from the jumble of things lying on Sushil's once-tidy desk. 'Look, I'm pretty grateful you gave me a place to stay and all that, but you manage your love life the way you like, and I'll manage mine, okay?'

'Okay,' Sushil said. 'And while we're on the subject...'

'You need me to move out?' Zina bit her lip. After she lost the room in Mrs Anthony's flat, Sushil was the first person she had thought of. She had met him at a party and they'd hit it off. Neither of them was in the market for a relationship just then—Sushil because he had gotten out of a turbulent relationship and was thinking of getting back with his wife, and Zina because she was engaged to Shiven. Sushil was lonely and Zina discovered pretty soon that hanging out with him was a safe and very effective way of keeping Shiven on the hop. Also, Sushil shared her love for expensive restaurants and was rich enough to foot the bill without blinking. Or expecting anything in return.

Being 'just good friends' was a new and novel experience for both of them—it wouldn't have worked if they'd been attracted to each other, but luckily they weren't. 'We're too similar,' Zina said one day, and with a twinge of alarm, Sushil realised she was right. Both of them had an effortless appeal for the opposite sex—they both were careless and a little unscrupulous about casual relationships, and they even shared their zodiac sign.

'Before Anjali shifts to Mumbai,' Sushil said. That was one way he and Zina were completely different, he thought triumphantly. He genuinely cared for Anjali and Gayatri, and so far, he hadn't figured out a single person or thing that Zina cared about.

'Does she know I'm here?' Zina asked curiously, and Sushil flushed. 'No,' he said. 'Not yet. I'm not even sure if I should tell her—it might be a bit too much for her to take in. What do you think I should do?'

God, he must be really desperate if he was asking her for advice, Zina thought. She found it faintly ridiculous; Sushil's sudden desire to reunite with a wife he had done perfectly well without for over a decade. This must be what a mid-life crisis looked like, she decided. Pity he had chosen to have one before she found a place to live.

There was a little pause, and then Zina said, 'You can tell her. Or not. Doesn't matter a bit to me, honestly. Probably doesn't matter to her either. I'll move out in a week or so, once I find a new place that isn't an absolute dump.' She went back to carefully buffing her nails, and Sushil glared at the back of her head in frustration. Honestly, either Zina was as thick as a plank, or she was deliberately trying to needle him.

'Zina, it matters to me,' he said, consciously keeping his temper under check. 'I really want Gayatri to have a stable home, and it's important that we figure this out.'

'Hmm...' Zina said, putting a nail file down and picking a bottle of clear nail varnish. 'Shh for a minute, I need to get the base coat right.'

'You work in a bloody beauty salon!' Sushil exploded. 'Why can't you do this stuff there?'

'Because Rehaan says it's unprofessional,' she said, her face darkening a little. 'Bloody slave-driver.' She finished one coat of polish and waggled her fingers in the air. 'Why're you getting so worked up anyway? And who's Gayatri? I thought your wife was called Anita or something like that.'

'Anjali.'

'Yes, whatever, same thing. So is Gayatri?'

'My daughter,' Sushil said through gritted teeth.

'Oh yes, the super brilliant one.' Zina frowned. 'Yeah, you should get her over here before that father-in-law of yours turns her into a geek no guy will look at twice. Believe it or not, I was going that way as a kid myself.' She gave a little shudder. 'Thank heavens for Femina and Stardust. I turned myself around just in time.'

Just in time to turn into a complete good-time girl, Sushil thought, suddenly feeling very grateful to Dr Mishra for bringing up Gayatri conservatively. Zina might be street-smart and ultra-sexy, but one thing she was not, was a role model any man would choose for his daughter.

'You know what, you should tell your wife,' Zina said. 'Nothing happened anyway, I just stayed in your guest bedroom for a week, and now I'm off.'

'I know nothing happened,' Sushil said patiently. 'I'm just not sure Anjali will see it the same way. And the neighbours are sure to talk.'

'Shift out of Bandra then,' Zina said shrugging her shoulders carelessly. 'Anyway there won't be enough space here for you and a wife and kid.' Sushil stared at her. His flat was the ultimate in swanky bachelor pads, but it wasn't large. For once, Zina actually seemed to have a point.

'Thanks,' he said slowly. 'That's exactly what I'll do. And this time, I'll get a flat with a sea-view.'

'What about this place then?' Zina turned her big brown eyes up at him. 'Can I stay on till your lease runs out?'

'If you can pay the rent and sort it with the landlord, yes,' Sushil said. 'If not, you'll need to find someplace else. I'll give you the landlord's number if you like.'

A week later, he was wishing he hadn't been quite so sarcastic. For a glorified hairdresser, Zina was very well-paid, but her salary was still half the rent of the flat. What Sushil hadn't reckoned with, was her powers of persuasion. Before he knew what was happening, he was being encouraged not-very-subtly by the landlord to move out because Zina had convinced him that she'd pay twenty per cent more than Sushil's company was paying.

'Where's the money coming from?' Sushil asked suspiciously. 'I don't want the landlord coming after me when you vanish without paying the rent.'

'It'll get paid, don't worry,' Zina said, and that was

all he could get out of her. Two days before he moved out, the hoarding in front of the building went back to advertising stupendously cheap holidays to Thailand. Zina was rearranging stuff around the flat with an air of suppressed excitement, every so often vanishing into her room to whisper into the phone with someone. Evidently she had found a new boyfriend who was rich enough to afford the rent. Sushil wondered why he felt so disappointed in Zina. It wasn't like he started out with any major illusions about her—the first time he met her, she had confessed to being with Shiven because he had 'a fat bank balance with no idea how to spend it'. Unfortunately, Shiven also had a habit of following Zina around like a lovesick Rottweiler, and finally the bank balance hadn't been big enough for her to stick with him.

'All the best in the new flat,' Zina said, leaning up to give Sushil a hug as the movers put the last of his stuff into the van. Clearly they thought he was being thrown out by his girlfriend, as all of them were now waiting discreetly by the gate as he said his goodbyes.

'I'll never get my street cred back,' Sushil said ruefully as he noticed a few neighbours peeking out of their windows. 'Not only do they think you've traded me in for a hotter, richer model, they're also feeling sorry for me because I'm out on the streets.'

'Never mind, you've got your wife and kid back at least,' Zina said, giving him a consoling pat. 'And once they figure out who I've traded you in for, they'll probably think you've had a lucky escape from a madwoman.'

Sushil raised his eyebrows, but Zina laughed and shook her head, her feathery hair fanning out over her shoulders with the movement. 'I'll tell you someday,' she said, her eyes alight with mischief. 'Right now, it's a secret.'

She looked so roguishly pretty that Sushil couldn't help himself—all his irritation vanished in an instant, and he bent and kissed her impulsively right on the lips. 'Take care of yourself,' he said, and turned to stride away towards his car, not noticing the arrested expression on Zina's face. The movers scuttled into the van with newfound respect in their eyes as they followed Sushil's car out of the lane. Zina stared after them for a minute, and then broke into a quick smile as she wiped her lips with the back of her hand. 'Some men are full of surprises,' she told the elderly Mrs Vaz who was hanging out her washing on the first-floor balcony. 'Pity he's married.' Ignoring Mrs Vaz's shocked expression, she went back into the building, humming the theme song from *Dhoom* as she climbed the stairs.

Sushil's new flat was in Mahalakshmi, overlooking the race course, and almost twice the size of the Bandra flat. For the first few days after he moved in, he came back there only to sleep—the flat made him uneasy, it was so clearly meant for a family. The day Anjali and Gayatri arrived, he ordered in lunch from a nearby Chinese restaurant before he went to pick them up from the airport. He was nervous, he realised, as he paced the covered area in front of the Arrivals terminal. And surprisingly, it wasn't nervousness about getting back to a normal marriage—one afternoon in bed with Anjali had left him wanting more. Besides, he was sick of serial relationships with demanding, pushy women. With Anjali, he felt a bit like the way he did when he sat down to a meal of daal-chawal-subzi at home after weeks of travelling and eating indigestible and unpronounceable food at five-star hotels.

What was getting the butterflies in his stomach to flutter around frantically was the thought of learning to be a full-time father to a twelve-year-old. Gayatri was so mature, she scared him at times. Anjali had told him once that she had faced trouble in school because her parents didn't live together. What if Gayatri held that against him? Worse, what if she thought of him as a bit of a buffoon? She was very close to Anjali's father, and the old man's long-held view was that Sushil's intellectual capabilities were only slightly higher than that of the average pigeon.

For a few seconds, he even contemplated offering to move to a hotel for a few weeks so that Anjali and Gayatri had some space. Then he looked up to see his wife and daughter stepping out of the door. Anjali was pushing a trolley loaded with suitcases, and she was trying to juggle her phone out of her bag, presumably to call Sushil. Gayatri, however, was looking straight ahead and she spotted Sushil almost instantly. She broke into a smile that was so guilelessly happy that Sushil's heart turned over with pride and joy. 'I'm so happy to see you guys,' he said, stepping up to Anjali and taking the trolley from her. Once he had steered it to a safe corner out of the way of other passengers, he took a deep breath and put an arm around each of his women, pulling them close for a hug. 'This might sound really corny, but I have to say it—welcome to Mumbai!'

Dear Nanaji,

Am e-mailing you as soon as we arrive like you told me to. I am using Papa's iPad—we are driving over the sea-link right now. The bridge is very pretty, but I can't make out what kind it is. I think it is cable, and not suspension. I will Google it and check.

I can't wait to see our new flat. Papa has a nice car. It's a BMW, and the driver drives very fast. Wish you were here!

Love,
Gayatri

three

'MOVIE NOT OVER yet?' Anjali asked as she walked into the TV room a few hours later. Sushil and Gayatri had been glued to the TV set since lunch while she tried to arrange stuff in the kitchen. When she had last walked into the room, the man on the screen was being dropped overboard into a sea of sharks. To make things more interesting, he had now been bound hand and foot to a busty bikini-clad beauty, and there'd been some complicated stuff happening with a rope tied around their collective ankles.

'He's still alive?' Anjali asked incredulously as she watched the same man single-handedly battle half a dozen baddies. Sushil gave her an impatient look. 'Of course he's alive,' he said. 'He's James Bond.'

Anjali squinted at the screen. Never a big fan of action movies, she had lost track of the Bonds. This wasn't Sean Connery, and it wasn't Pierce Brosnan either. And the movie looked old, it couldn't be what's-his-name, the steely-eyed blond guy who'd played Bond in the last few movies.

'It's Roger Moore,' Sushil said without looking up. 'Really, Anjali. Didn't you have cable TV at your Dad's place?'

'We watched BBC and Discovery Channel on it,' she retorted. It was true, but when her father wasn't home, she usually tuned to Bollywood channels to watch re-runs of Madhuri Dikshit movies. Leaning across, she picked up the packet of chips Sushil was eating and said, 'I thought you said you were going to eat healthy?'

'There has to be something healthy to eat,' Sushil muttered. There had been one problem after another with getting the kitchen up and running. First, he discovered that the building didn't have piped gas, and it took days for a new gas connection. Just when that got sorted, the brand-new refrigerator died on him, and all the vegetables inside rotted into a horrible slimy mess. Today was the first day that the kitchen was actually stocked and functioning.

'I'll get started with dinner in a few minutes,' Anjali said. 'Alu-gobhi and matar-paneer okay by you?'

'Sounds perfect,' he said. 'But you don't need to stress yourself out with cooking every day—we'll hire a cook.'

Anjali stared at him. 'A cook for what?' she said. 'I used to do the cooking every day for Dad and Gayatri and that was when I was working full-time. What'll I do all day?' 'Go back to work, maybe?' Sushil suggested. 'Once we've got Gayatri admitted to a decent school.'

Anjali made a face. 'I don't want to teach anymore,' she said. 'Mumbai kids are all so brash and noisy, and *pimply*. I'll have to find something else to do.'

'Pimply, eh?' Sushil laughed. 'Not like Indore kids?'

'Not like Indore kids at all,' Anjali said, hesitating a little before she plopped onto the floor next to him. 'It'd be nice to take a break for a bit actually. Get used to Mumbai, help Gayatri settle into school. Unless you think…'

'Take a break by all means,' Sushil said. 'I think you'll get bored pretty quick though—I know you. But we can talk about it again once Gayatri's school admission is done.'

Gayatri had studied in one of the best schools in Indore, but Mumbai schools seemed to be an entirely different ball-game. Anjali had expected that Gayatri would need to go through an entrance exam, and had been secretly coaching her ever since she knew they were moving. What she hadn't expected was that she and Sushil would be interviewed as well.

'Wellington is a niche school,' one of her neighbours explained. 'And it's run by a board of trustees who are very particular about keeping the ethos of the school alive. There are over a hundred applications for each vacancy, so they can afford to pick and choose.'

'Why can't we apply to some of the regular schools as well?' Anjali demanded when Sushil got home in the evening. 'Why only two?' Sushil had got application forms for Wellington and for another school that was less well-known, but apparently had amazing facilities.

Sushil shrugged. 'I think Wellington would be the best for her,' he said. 'Cathedral and J. B. Petit don't have vacancies in her age-group, else I'd have tried there as well.'

Anjali picked up the second set of forms. 'What about this one then? EduVista?' The brochure that accompanied the forms was glossy and showed a bunch of happy, healthy-looking children working at computers, painting murals and playing football. She turned to the last page and blinked in disbelief—the fees were considerably higher than what she'd made in her teaching job.

'Sushil? Have you seen the fees?'

Sushil looked a little annoyed, and walked across the room to take the brochure from her. 'Don't worry about the fees,' he said. 'My office will take care of it. In any case, that's the back-up school. It's new, and my company has a deal with the management—we'll get preference over other applicants. But Wellington is what we should gun for.'

On the day of the Wellington interview, Anjali felt unaccountably nervous. Partly because Sushil had taken it upon himself to drill her for the parents' interview, and issued a set of contradictory instructions every day. 'They like the mothers to be confident and outgoing,' he said one day. The next day, he had evidently had a re-think. 'Maybe you should let me handle the questions,' he said, his forehead furrowed up in thought. 'I'll bring you into the conversation when it's required.'

Now, as they waited outside the interview room, he hissed at her, 'Think before you talk, okay? Don't blurt out the first thing that comes into your head.'

The interview panel was far less forbidding than Anjali had expected. There were two men; one, a plump, fatherly-looking man in his forties who introduced himself as the head of the Admissions Committee. The other man was younger, lean and quiet. The woman was the most intimidating of the lot—sharp-featured, with a spiky haircut and spectacles with thick, bright-blue frames, she looked like she had stepped out of a TV show. Not a saas-bahu one either, but the kind where intellectuals discussed economics and world politics.

The first few questions were ordinary enough, and as they'd decided, Sushil answered most of them. Then the sharp-faced lady leaned forward.

'Mrs Dubey, I have a question for you.'

Anjali nodded, hoping she didn't look too apprehensive. The woman—she had introduced herself as Kavita Subramanian—looked down at their application form.

'When I read through what you've written about your daughter, she seems to have a lot of different interests. Reading, singing, gymnastics...even pottery, I see. What do you think she'd best suited to do when she grows up?'

It sounded like a trick question, and Anjali took a few

seconds to think before she answered. 'I'd like her to take that decision,' she said slowly. 'But if you're asking for my opinion, I think she's most suited to be a teacher.'

Clearly Kavita wasn't interested in Anjali's opinion because she hardly listened to the second part of her answer.

'So let's say, she completes school and isn't able to decide,' she said. 'And she wants to take a gap year and travel around the world before she makes up her mind about college and a career. Would you be okay with that?'

Sushil opened his mouth to say something, but Kavita held up a well-shaped but slightly bony hand. 'Anjali?' she said, as Anjali hesitated.

'I suppose the "correct" answer is that I'd let her take the year off,' she said slowly. 'But honestly, I'd tell her to finish college and get a job and travel around the world with her own money once she's saved up enough.'

She could feel the waves of disbelief coming off Sushil, but she didn't look at him. Kavita was nodding gravely, a bit like a doctor seeing a new disease for the first time.

'I'd like to understand this a little better,' she said, steepling her fingers together so that her diamond rings glittered under the overhead light. 'Would you say no to the gap year because of the money it would cost? Or because you feel that it's irresponsible to take a year off?'

'Neither, actually,' Anjali said. 'I feel that it's our duty as parents to make sure that our child has every possible opportunity. But in turn, the child has a duty to make the best use of those opportunities. Taking a year off is a bit of a waste.'

'Isn't a gap year one of those opportunities that privileged parents like you can provide your child?' It was the first question the quiet-looking man had asked so far, and something about his expression made Anjali think that he was genuinely interested in her answer.

'It's something we can afford,' Anjali admitted. 'But it's not something my daughter can or should demand of us as a right. In my view, she'll get far more out of a gap year that she's worked and saved up for, than if her father pays for it.'

'What if she took on an evening job and saved up for the gap year while she was in school?' Kavita asked.

'I'd definitely be more open to it.'

'Great,' Kavita said briskly. 'So that's all that we wanted to ask. Do you have any questions for us?'

Sushil asked a few politically correct questions about the curriculum and the teaching methods, and they said their goodbyes.

Anjali gave Sushil an apprehensive look once they were out of the school. 'I'm sorry,' she said. 'I messed up, didn't I?'

She had expected him to be annoyed, but surprisingly, he laughed, shaking his head. 'It's fine,' he said, putting an arm around her shoulders. 'You were honest, and who knows, maybe it'll make us stand out from the rest of the applicants. If we don't get through, there's always EduVista.'

Still, Anjali spent the rest of the week going around with a heavy feeling in the pit of her stomach. If they didn't get through, Sushil—or, okay, his office—would have to pay a small fortune to EduVista, and she knew she'd feel guilty for as long as Gayatri stayed in the school. Without telling Sushil, she even did some research into schools in the area, coming up with the same depressing facts. The good schools had no vacancies, and the others were as expensive as EduVista.

'Put her in the nearest Kendriya Vidyalaya,' her father grunted when she tried to explain the problem to him over the phone. 'It was good enough for you and Sushil, wasn't it? And it'll cost much less.'

There wasn't any arguing with that, and Anjali gave up before her father could branch off into a lecture on her extravagant big-city ways.

Dear Nanaji,

I got admission into Wellington School. Mummy said it's a very good school, but the building is much smaller than my old school. They teach Marathi instead of Sanskrit and we also need to learn French. I think I will need French tuition.

Our new flat is very nice. It's big and on the 16th floor, and you can see the sea from one side of the house and the train station from the other. It's in Mahalakshmi. When will you visit us? The balcony is very big.

Mummy is looking for a job, but she doesn't want to teach in a college. I hope she finds something interesting.

Love,
Gayatri

four

ZINA TWIRLED AROUND in front of the mirror, the overhead lights in the salon making the sequins on her corset top sparkle. The top had been reduced to half-price in an end-of-season sale, and Zina was very proud of it.

'Very nice,' her boss said drily, coming out of his office just as she was smoothing her hands over her floor-length multi-layered chiffon skirt. 'Now if you've quite finished admiring yourself, perhaps you could tell me why you overcharged Mrs Kapadia for her hair-straightening treatment?'

'Because she's a stupid, stuck-up bitch, and I hate her,' Zina said. 'Honestly, the amount of time she wasted fussing over her hair length and the kind of treatment she wanted, I should have charged her twice as much.'

'Hmm,' Rehaan said. 'Real reason, please?'

Zina frowned, and flopped into one of the swivelling chairs. 'I billed her for permanent re-bonding by mistake,' she said. 'But seriously, Rehaan, she was being such a pain, going on and on, and Suzy wasn't around either. I got distracted and clicked the wrong code by mistake. It's that software, you should speak to the guys who sold it to you, the drop-down menus are a mess...'

'Let's face it, the only kind of menus you can handle are the kind you find in restaurants,' Rehaan said. 'From now on, if Suzy's busy, just call me and I'll handle the billing. Right now, we need to sort this mess out.'

'You can give her a big discount the next time she comes here,' Zina said hopefully. Rehaan gave her a look. 'Zina, she's so upset she's threatening to call up some politician she knows and get the salon shut down. I don't think a discount is going to work. What you need to do is go over to her place, refund the money for the entire treatment, and give her this gift hamper. And apologise profusely.' He held up a hand as Zina began to protest. 'Or, you can go find yourself another job. I mean it, Zina.' Zina shut her mouth and glumly took the hamper from him. 'I was going out tonight,' she said grumpily.

'You can go after you've met Mrs Kapadia and grovelled a bit.' He waited till she reached the door of the salon and said, 'And Zina?'

She turned, her eyebrows raised inquiringly.

'The TV thing worked out.'

'You mean—am I—seriously? Oh wow!!! Rehaan, that's fabulous news!' Dumping Mrs Kapadia's expensive hamper onto the floor, she darted back and threw her arms around him in an exuberant hug. 'The TV thing' was a reality show on makeovers that Rehaan had been working on with an entertainment channel, and he had asked Zina to be his on-screen assistant. She had done a few screen-tests and she thought they had gone pretty well, even though they insisted she speak in Hindi, and her accent wasn't all that good. Because of her short stint as a model, she was comfortable in front of the camera, and she knew she looked good. Still, weeks had gone by without any news. For a bit, even Rehaan had become pessimistic, wondering if they were cancelling the show altogether. But now, he was grinning all over his face as he hugged her back.

'You'll need to work really hard,' he warned. 'No goofing around with the cameraman or staying home pretending to be ill.'

'I'll be very, very, good,' she promised. 'I'll even work overtime if you pay me enough.'

Feeling a lot more pleased with life, Zina got into a cab and gave the cabbie the address. The salon was on Peddar Road, and Mrs Kapadia lived in Mahalakshmi, not too far from the club Zina was going to for dinner. When she wanted to, Zina could be very charming—by the time she was done apologising, Mrs Kapadia was completely mollified, even asking her to stay back and have something to eat.

'I'll come by some other time,' Zina said, giving her a bright smile and edging into the lift. 'Bye, have a nice evening!'

Once the lift doors shut, she sagged against the corner. Damn, being polite was stressful. And now she was late for the party—the guy who'd invited her had said they'd meet at the bar at around 7.30 for cocktails, and it would be a quarter to nine before she reached. She was drumming her fingers impatiently against the wall when the lift gave a sudden little jerk and came to a juddering halt. For a second, Zina stared stupidly at the closed doors and then began jabbing at the buttons on the panel. Nothing worked, and when she pulled her phone out of her bag, she figured that the signal wasn't strong enough for her to make a call. The only thing left to do, was to try the call button in the lift panel, but the phone rang without anyone picking up. Presumably it rang in the security guard's cabin, and the security guard was doing more interesting things than hanging around there waiting for people to call him.

'Okay, this seriously sucks,' Zina muttered as she tried to get her phone to work. The phone stubbornly refused to oblige, and she gave up, and flung it back into her bag. 'Here goes,' she said, taking a deep breath and hammering against the lift doors. Nothing happened. 'Hello?' she called out. 'Anyone there? I'm...umm...stuck in the lift.' For a moment she contemplated yelling 'Bachao, bachao,' but that would have been too Bollywood-ish for words. On the other hand, there seemed a good chance she'd be stuck here for the rest of the night. Feeling slightly desperate, she hammered on the door again, giving it a few kicks for good measure.

'Mom, there's someone stuck in the lift!' a young voice said, and Zina sagged against the wall in relief. Thank heavens for kids and their sharp ears. An older voice said, 'Wait, I'll call the security guard on the intercom.'

It still took a few minutes for the security guard to land up, but Zina was quite happy to wait. The nameless woman had called out to her reassuringly a few times, and there were some pulling and grating noises that suggested that something was being done to get the doors open.

'Are you all right?' the woman asked as the security guard finally managed to pull the doors open. 'I'm good,' Zina said, registering with dismay that the lift was stuck between two floors. The top half of the lift was in the shaft, and the bottom half was suspended five feet above a landing. The guard and the woman who'd spoken to her were peering up at her looking worried.

'Madam...' the guard began to say, and suddenly ground to a halt looking confused. He was in his early twenties, and the sight of Zina in her sequinned top, bare shoulders and flowing skirt was a bit too much for his village-reared sensibilities. The woman took over. 'Can you jump down?' she asked.

Zina gave the drop a dubious look. 'I could,' she said. 'But the instructions in the lift say that you shouldn't try to climb out.'

'You'll be jumping down, not climbing out,' the girl who'd originally raised the alarm said. She looked older than Zina had thought from her voice—she was taller than her mother, and had to be at least twelve or thirteen. 'And Yadavji has put the main switch off. The lift won't start up and cut you in half if that's what you're worried about.'

'Gayatri!' her mother said crossly. 'You can come down, I think it's quite safe.'

It was all very well for her to say it was quite safe to jump, but Zina didn't fancy the thought of breaking a leg.

'I'll call Papa,' the girl decided, and turning, she ran into her flat. Zina plonked herself on the floor of the lift and prepared to wait a little longer. Yadavji looked quite eager to help out, only she was quite certain from the way he was looking at her that a Bhojpuri dream sequence was playing out in his mind. The girl's dad would be a safer bet.

'This is the third time the lift's conked this week,' a male voice said, and Zina crept to the edge and peered down. The man looked up, and an exasperated expression crossed his ruggedly handsome face.

'I don't believe this,' he said. 'Zina, you're only some four feet from the ground. Here, take my hand and jump.'

'Let me chuck my shoes down first,' Zina said, throwing her precious new neon-orange wedges out of the lift for Gayatri to catch. Then she took Sushil's hand and slithered down.

'Thanks,' she said, beaming at him. 'Won't you introduce me to your family?'

'Let me get this straight,' Anjali said slowly once Zina had left. 'You were actually living with this woman?' Zina hadn't bothered being discreet, and it had taken about two seconds for her to spill everything.

Sushil groaned. 'She was living in the same flat as me, yes. Was I sleeping with her? No. And before you say it, I know you only have my word for it.' He was feeling positively murderous towards Zina. She hadn't even tried to be discreet, and it had taken Anjali about two seconds to figure out that Zina and he had shared a flat for almost a month.

'Stop getting upset,' Anjali said. 'I'm asking because I'm curious, and I'm wondering why you were so secretive about the whole thing.'

'It wasn't something I could just blurt out when I was asking you to move back with me, could I?'

Anjali tried to imagine the conversation. 'Honey, I'd really like us to be together again, except, hang on, I've to get rid of this girl who just happens to be living with me... No, there's nothing happening, she's just an out-of-work actress who needed a place to stay...' Hmm, he was right.

'When we were...separated,' she said. 'There was someone else, right?'

Sushil bit his lip. He knew this would come up some time, and the last thing he wanted was to feel guilty about it. 'Yes,' he said, bottling down the excuses that automatically came bubbling up. He had been lonely, his wife was in a different country and anyway, even when they were in the same country, they couldn't spend an hour together without fighting. Of course he had found someone else.

'So what happened?' she asked, and she sounded more curious than upset.

Sushil shrugged. 'We were together for a while. It was sort of fizzling out anyway after the first few months, and she got transferred out of the Middle East around then, so we split up.' It was partly true, and he didn't feel the need to mention that he came very close to asking for a divorce so that he could marry Shalini. Luckily he found out in time how possessive and controlling Shalini could be and broken it off.

'Right now I think we should forget about what's happened and concentrate on the future,' Sushil said, hoping he didn't sound like a politician after a real-estate scam. 'After all, you had that Khatri chap dangling behind you—I haven't been questioning you about him, have I?'

'If you thought I'd come within touching distance of him, you'd have broken a few of his bones,' Anjali said. 'But point taken. I'll stay off your women if you promise to stop making stupid jokes about Deven.'

Zina wasn't enjoying the party at all. She had come because one of her banker friends had insisted, but she was bored out of her skull. The music was good, but no one in her group was dancing—all they seemed to like doing was knocking back drinks and stand around talking about money. And not money in terms of 'oooh how lovely it was!' and the amazing things one could buy with it, but instead how you should invest it and what percentage of your capital you should use for what and so on. It was all very dreary, and the guy who'd invited her was the dreariest of them all. The women were even worse, but they were thankfully all ugly, and Zina ignored them

'Having fun, babes?' Zina turned towards Satyen, hilariously called Steve by his friends, and shook her head firmly. 'I've never been so bored in my life,' she said. To her surprise, Steve laughed. 'You're amazing,' he said. 'Isn't she amazing, guys?' Clearly he was more than a little drunk, and Zina leaned away from him. 'You bet I am,' she said, scanning the room over his shoulder for someone even slightly more interesting.

'Hey, I just saw someone I know,' she said, gently pushing Steve away. 'I'll be back in a minute, okay?'

To be on the safe side, she picked up her little clutch purse. If possible, she'd make her getaway directly afterwards and send Steve a message saying she had just heard her grandmother died or something. What a waste of an evening! And poor granny, this was the fourth time she'd meet an untimely end this year.

She was halfway to the door when a voice said lazily, 'Leaving so soon?' Her eyebrows arched up as she turned to see the speaker. 'Do I know you?'

'Not yet,' he said, getting to his feet in a single fluid movement. 'But that's easily fixed. Amazing skirt, by the way.'

Zina had made the skirt herself, though she would have died before admitting to doing something as uncool as sewing, and she was flattered enough to look at the man more closely. Okay, man was a bit of an over-statement. Boy was more like it, because he couldn't have been more than twenty. Just a little taller than her, with flashing eyes, a fabulous, sardonic-looking mouth and jet-black hair flopping untidily over his forehead, he was quite amazingly good-looking. Good-looking enough for Zina to pause a few seconds before she asked, 'Does your mom know you're out on your own?'

'Yes, she even ironed my shirt for me before I left.' He put a confident hand on the small of her back as he opened the door to usher her out of the pub, and Zina felt an automatic little thrill go through her. There was something about the boy's natural confidence that put her normally sassy tongue on standby.

'D'you like sushi?' the boy asked once they were outside. 'Hate it,' Zina said succinctly. Her one experience with sushi had been when Rehaan had brought a bento box into the salon for them to share. She almost gagged on the seaweed covering.

'Oh well, we'll go to the Hard Rock Cafe then,' he said. 'My car's parked just behind the pub. Or we could walk if you like.'

'Look, kiddo, I don't remember agreeing to go anywhere with you,' Zina protested. 'And only crazy people walk around in this area after dark.'

'Car then,' he said, and Zina found herself following him. It occurred to her on the way that only crazy people got into cars with strange men, but he was so *young*, it was almost ridiculous thinking of him as a threat.

His car was a surprise—she had expected a Santro, or at the most, a Honda City. The sleek BMW with silver trimmings stopped her in her tracks.

'It's my mom's,' he said, as he clicked the remote to open the doors. 'Once she finished ironing my shirt, I asked if I could borrow it.' As Zina hesitated before approaching the car, he turned to her and took out his wallet. For an awful second, she thought he was about to give her money, then she saw he was pulling out his driver's licence. 'I think you should see some form of identification,' he said seriously. 'Before you get in the car.'

'Ishaan Mehta' the license said, and in the photo, he looked even younger than he did in real life. Zina glanced at his date of birth before handing the license back. She had been right—he was a couple of months short of twenty one.

'If you're planning to strangle me and dump me in the sea, knowing your name won't help,' Zina said, but she couldn't deny that she felt a lot safer. Being impulsive was one thing, being downright stupid was another, and she had a feeling that she was tending towards the latter.

He gave her a quick smile, his sculpted lips curving up at the corners. 'You could message the details to someone,' he pointed out. 'And not to be unchivalrous, but you're almost the same size as I am—strangling you might pose some technical difficulties.'

The Hard Rock Cafe was noisy and full of people, but Ishaan managed to get them a table in a corner. 'Now, tell me all about yourself,' he said, turning the full force of his sexy eyes onto Zina. 'How did you end up with Steve and his bunch of banker-wankers?'

'Met Steve at a party a month ago,' Zina said. 'He seemed pretty okay then. Definitely not as boring as he was today.'

'His scriptwriter must be on leave,' Ishaan said solemnly. 'The next time you go out with a guy, you should do a few basic checks.'

'Like?'

'Footwear for one,' Ishaan said. 'If the guy wears trainers with jeans, he's probably the engineer-MBA-banker type. Total nerd, totally avoidable. And his ringtone—let's face it, Steve's was hideous.'

Zina put her head to one side. 'So what kind of guy should I go for?' 'Please don't say guys like you,' she begged him mentally. That would spoil it all—she hated guys who were over-confident.

Ishaan gave her an impish grin. 'Oh, definitely the caveman type,' he said. 'One of those tall, hairy-chested men who'd terrify the world but would be your abject slave.'

He'd described Shiven to a T, and Zina felt a little frisson of worry. The boy was way too perceptive. And now he made her wonder whether he wasn't really interested in her after all—perhaps he had just decided to detach her from her group to prove that he could do it. Her eyes narrowed a little as she looked at him. He was as different from the description he had given of her ideal man as Shahid Kapoor was from Dara Singh. He wasn't tall, and from what she could see of his chest through the open collar of his shirt, he wasn't terribly hairy either. And as for being her abject slave, he didn't look the type to be anyone's slave, abject or otherwise...

'Pretty much the man of my dreams,' she said, sighing dreamily in response to his description. 'Oh well, until I find him, I guess I'll have to make do with what's available.'

Luckily, what was available was pretty hot stuff. And kissing Ishaan posed no 'technical difficulties' at all. In fact, being almost the same height helped, because there was none of that awkward, tiptoeing and bending down business; she just had to lean forward a little, and the instinct she had when she'd first set eyes on his perfect mouth, was correct. He was fantastic at kissing, and at a lot else, and his body was about as perfect as his mouth and his eyes...

'D'you live with your mom?' she asked him after a bit. 'The one who irons your shirts and lends you her car,' she added, because his eyes were a bit unfocussed after the kiss.

'Yes,' he said, smiling a little as her hands roved over him hungrily. 'Unfortunately. And she's at home tonight.

All her geriatric boyfriends are out of town.'

'Okay, my place then,' she said, and he nodded obediently, though there was nothing obedient in the way he pulled her back into his arms. And absolutely nothing obedient at all in the way he made love to her all night long—at some point, it occurred to her that she was probably a terrible person, bringing him back to a flat that was paid for by another man. Then his mouth came down on hers again, and she pushed the thought to a corner of her mind.

Dear Nanaji,

Thanks for your e-mail, and sorry to hear that you weren't well. Are you okay now? Mom spoke to Arvind Mama, and he said you were back home.
Today the lift got stuck and we had to help an aunty out. She was very pretty.
I will start at my new school tomorrow. I'm a little nervous, but I plan to work very hard, especially in the new subjects.
When are you coming to Mumbai?

Love,
Gayatri

five

'IT JUST DOESN'T seem worth it, does it?' Anjali said. She had spent the last month applying for different kinds of jobs, right from research technician at a pharma company to admin head at a bank. The only one that had worked out was in Navi Mumbai, and it was so far away as to practically be in a different city. Plus the salary they were offering was only slightly higher than what Anjali paid her cook.

'Look, I know you. You won't be happy unless you're doing something,' Sushil said. 'Maybe not teach in a college, if you don't want to do that any longer, but there are dozens of other things you could try. There's no hurry—like you said, we don't need the money. Don't give up, that's all.'

'Hmm,' was all Anjali said, but she couldn't help thinking that it was easy for Sushil to dispense global gyan. So far he had provided very little practical help in finding a job. 'What should I wear for this office do of yours?' she asked. 'Churidaar-kameez okay?'

'Uhhh, most of the women will be wearing dresses,' Sushil said. 'Or jeans with dressy tops.'

'So I'll wear churidaar-kameez then,' Anjali said brightly, and Sushil groaned to himself. Wearing churidaar-kameez on every possible formal occasion had become Anjali's way of asserting her individuality. Not that it mattered really, but she looked rather nice in jeans and even better in the dresses he got her during his last trip to the US. And she wore jeans whenever she could in Indore.

Today's outfit was black (good), with silver embroidery (not so good), and cut in the Anarkali style (absolutely not good). Anjali looked lovely, but a bit like she was about to plonk onto a divan and start singing 'Salaam-e-Ishq'. He almost told her so, then realised that he'd just be putting a new idea into her head. Honestly, she was as bad as Zina in some ways.

'I don't know why your office guys don't invite the full family to parties,' she was saying now, and Sushil looked up in surprise. 'But they have...oh you mean Gayatri?'

'Yes, I mean Gayatri,' Anjali said tersely, and Sushil had a sudden light-bulb moment. So *that* was why Anjali was so prickly about any get-together organised by his colleagues. She had effectively been a single mom for so many years that she thought of herself and her daughter as an indivisible unit, and she resented Gayatri's exclusion.

'You know, I don't think Gayatri wants to come along,' Sushil said gently. 'She's quite happy at home, watching TV and reading. And Lalita's around so it's not like she's alone. Gayatri probably looks forward to evenings when we're away.'

Anjali's tense expression lightened as she admitted, 'Yes, she does. Lalita and she watch music videos and Gayatri stays up till twelve or twelve-thirty... I'm sorry Sushil, this whole couple thing just feels so *weird* at times. I've got so used to being alone.'

Sushil crossed the room to her and gave her a swift kiss. 'You'll get used to it,' he said. 'I'm just as bad. My boss asked me the other day how "Mrs Dubey" was, and I was about to tell him that my mother's dead when I figured out he meant you. Come on, let's go.'

If Zina and Anjali could have compared notes on the world's most boring parties, it would have been difficult to choose between the one hosted by Sushil's company and the party Zina had fled from two nights ago. Zina had at least found a hot man to run away with—Anjali found herself stuck with the firm's Swedish finance head. Erik Larsen was tall and weedy, and as unimpressive looking as a human being could be without turning into a vegetable. Even his white skin wasn't a redeeming factor, Anjali noticed, feeling sorry for him but wishing devoutly that he'd find someone else to talk to. Painfully shy, his only topic of conversation seemed to be the trouble he was having adjusting to Mumbai.

'I'm trying to learn Hindi,' he said earnestly. 'But the guy I'm learning from—he just speaks too fast. I don't even understand his English...'

Erik himself spoke verrrryyy verrrryyy slooooowly—at several points in the conversation, Anjali felt like shaking him to make him complete a sentence. Natural politeness was all very well, but Erik's speech delivery reminded her of a soda-water bottle held upside down. 'Glug...glug... glug' about summed it up.

'Should I be jealous?' Sushil murmured into her ear as he passed. 'Larsen's sticking to you like he's auditioning for a Fevicol ad.'

Anjali gritted her teeth. Erik was boring, but he was also nice, and Sushil hadn't bothered to keep his voice down. It was sheer luck Erik hadn't heard—he was busy getting her a drink.

'Thanks,' she said when he came back.

'"Dhanyawad," is what they say for "thank you", isn't it?' Erik asked earnestly. 'But everyone gives me weird looks when I try to say it. Am I pronouncing it wrong or something?'

'No, you're not,' Anjali said. 'It's just that it's not commonly used. Even when someone's speaking in Hindi, they'd say "Thanks" instead of using the Hindi word.'

'See, that's the kind of thing my teacher isn't able to explain,' Erik said. 'You know, I bet you'd make a brilliant teacher.'

Erik's words came back to Anjali as she attended a quiz show in Gayatri's school the next day. One round was in Hindi, and it was frankly appalling, the way the kids struggled through it. And the parents were worse, if anything. Some had good reasons for their pathetic Hindi—some were South Indians, or Bengalis, and in one case, British— but the rest seemed to be actually proud of not knowing the language.

'What would you call your mother's sister?' the Hindi teacher asked into the mic. Her expression suggested that she'd be eternally grateful if one of the kids got it right, but wouldn't bet on it.

'Aunty,' one of the fathers in the audience said firmly. 'That's what I'd call my mom's sister.'

'Chachi?' the kid answering the question hazarded, and Anjali looked up in amazement. The teacher looked resigned, and her smile had a gritted-teeth effect. 'Sorry, wrong answer,' she said. 'The question passes to the next team.'

Gayatri's team was up next, and Gayatri was pushed to the front.

'Mousi,' she said, and her house immediately got a point much to her team-mates' delight. The Hindi teacher brightened up as well. 'What about your father's sister?'

'Aunty again,' the man in the audience said triumphantly, and Anjali glared at him. He was a good-looking chap in his late thirties and he grinned back at her, completely unrepentant. The next few Hindi questions were a lot tougher, and they ended up with Gayatri as well, after being passed by the other teams.

'That girl's good,' Anjali heard one of the other parents say. 'New, isn't she?' The other mother nodded. 'Must find out where she goes for Hindi coaching,' she said. 'I pay my lady one thousand per class, and Krish can't string a single sentence together.'

The man who'd been answering every question with 'Aunty' came up to Anjali and asked, 'Are you the Hindi whiz-kid's mom?'

Anjali nodded. 'Amar Patel,' he said holding his hand out. 'I must compliment you. Your daughter's brilliant. I gave the kids a talk on computers last week, and she asked some really good questions. And her Hindi, of course, is brilliant.'

'Thanks,' Anjali said. 'I can't take any credit though—she gets her brains from my dad.'

'And her looks from you,' the man said, smiling down at her. Anjali was wearing a new neon-green shirt with white capri trousers and her hair was spilling over her shoulders in sexy disarray. She knew she looked good, but an extra compliment was always welcome.

'Thanks again,' she said, smiling up at him sunnily. The two mothers who'd been discussing Hindi coaching classes turned. 'You're such a flirt, Amar,' one of them scolded. 'Wait till I tell Saloni. Though I must say I agree with him,' she went on, turning to Anjali. 'You're both so pretty, you and your daughter. And I love her hair—it's so long and thick. My daughter's been pestering me for years to let her grow her hair, but it's so thin, her plaits look like bits of string.'

The other mom had been giving Anjali a complete once-over, and she said briskly, 'Now, you must tell me. How's her Hindi so good?'

'We've just moved here from Indore,' Anjali said apologetically—clearly the woman was expecting an overnight solution. 'Pretty much everyone speaks good Hindi there.'

'Indore,' Amar said thoughtfully. 'That's where...UP? No, hang on, MP, right?'

'MP,' Anjali said.

'Yessss! Geography was my favourite subject in school!' He gave her a happy, schoolboyish grin. 'So, what's it like there?'

'Umm...like any other place I suppose,' Anjali said, a bit nonplussed. What was he expecting, a short discourse on Central India?

'Your English is excellent as well,' the first woman said, and Amar laughed. 'I assume they teach English in schools there,' he said, redeeming himself in Anjali's eyes. 'See you then ladies, I've got places to be, deals to crack.'

When Sushil got home that evening, he found Anjali poring over something on her laptop. 'New business idea?' he asked lightly. This had happened a few times before when Anjali had been bitten by the entrepreneurship bug and spent hours researching an idea before finally deciding it wouldn't work.

'Sort of,' Anjali said, snapping the computer shut. 'I'm going to start Hindi classes.'

After his initial surprise, Sushil had to admit it made sense. Anjali was still wary of teaching kids though. 'I'd prefer to work with adults,' she said. 'People like Erik maybe, and that annoying guy whose son goes to Gayatri's school.'

'I knew it was all about Erik,' Sushil said sorrowfully. 'Ever since you've seen him, you've been thinking about him, figuring out ways in which the two of you could be together...' He laughed as Anjali threw a cushion at him. 'Sorry,' he said. 'It's a brilliant idea, Anjali—go for it.'

Quite predictably, Erik ended up being Anjali's first student. Better still, he roped in a few of his expat friends for the Saturday morning classes that Anjali started off with. There was Bill Sweeney, an American banker, and Lydia Dubova, the Russian wife of an Indian research scientist, both of whom who signed up immediately, and a few more who called Anjali saying they were interested. Like Erik, Bill and Lydia were more interested in picking up conversational Hindi rather than the bookish stuff, and planning the lessons for them was fun and challenging at the same time. Anjali got them to call the banks and navigate through the Hindi options on the IVR; she took them to Bollywood movies and got them to learn the lyrics to the songs. She even arranged a discussion with a government official who'd recently been transferred to Maharashtra from UP.

Zina found out about the classes from Lydia, who was one of Rehaan's most faithful customers. Once she got the details, she landed up at Anjali's flat after work, demanding to be allowed to join.

Anjai stared at her. 'You want to take Hindi classes?' she asked finally. 'Why?'

Zina flipped her hair over one shoulder. 'Because I can't speak the language well, that's why,' she explained in tones that suggested that she thought Anjali to be extraordinarily dim-witted.

'I figured that,' Anjali said drily. 'I meant, why from me?'

'Why not?' Zina said. 'It's convenient, and I know you have a vacant slot. And there's this TV thing. I'm not sure if I told you about it, but to do it properly, I need to learn quick. I can't afford to faff around.'

Zina *had* told her about it in detail, on the day she was rescued from the lift. Sometimes, Anjali wished Gayatri had just left her in the lift—someone would have rescued her eventually, and at least she wouldn't keep turning up like a bad penny.

'You'll have to work hard,' Anjali warned. 'Tell me a bit more about this show of yours—do you need to learn lines by heart, or do you just need to able to speak Hindi fluently?'

'My boss's got an offer to do this new reality show on surprise makeovers for people. Like, people will phone in and give names of their friends who they think need a makeover—Rehaan will choose some of them, and then he and the TV crew will land up and take someone normal-looking like, like...'

'Like me,' Anjali supplied, and Zina nodded vigorously. 'Yes, someone like you—you know, who's not particular about make-up or getting facials done and that kind of stuff, and then he and this team of fitness experts work on that person and try and make her look really glamorous, you know? For three months. And they get a modelling contract with one of the sponsors.'

'And where do you come in?'

'Right now, I just hover in the background and hand Rehaan stuff,' Zina admitted. 'But that'll change. I just need to be ready for when it does.'

Presumably, the guys who make the show would be bowled over by how well Zina passed the scissors and swept hair trimmings off the floor, Anjali thought bitchily. She hated the thought of giving Zina lessons, but she couldn't think of a single plausible reason to say no.

'Umm, in case you're wondering if I slept with your husband, no I didn't,' Zina offered. 'He's not my type. I like classy guys, you know, the aristocratic type. Tall and snooty-looking.' For aristocratic, read 'rich', Anjai thought but didn't say it. Zina continued, completely oblivious to what Anjali's reactions might be. 'Sushil's... he's cute, but he's very earthy, isn't he? I don't mean he's like a *villager* or anything. Just, umm...'

'Not your type, ' Anjali suggested. 'Lucky he's mine, then.'

'I guess,' Zina said, and then she broke into a smile. 'I don't think I'm his type either,' she confided. 'He was interested in the beginning, just a little, but then he started saying I'm too random. So will you teach me Hindi then?'

Not having come up with a good enough excuse, Anjali found herself writing Zina's name down in her students' register. So far, the register had only three names in it, but what the heck, Zina didn't need to know that.

'Saturday mornings at ten,' Anjali said. 'Don't forget. In case class gets cancelled any day, I'll message you.'

Sushil was disgusted when he heard. 'She's going to be on the screen for about five minutes in which she's going to be passing the scissors to her boss. Which, let's face it, shouldn't be extraordinarily difficult. It's unlikely she'll become the next Shweta Tiwari if she takes Hindi classes.'

'I was wondering…' Anjali said tentatively, 'Where will she get the money from to pay for the classes? They're not cheap, not with the prices you told me to quote for Erik.'

'She'll get one of her latest boyfriends to pay,' he said. 'Or her boss. And if she doesn't pay up, feel free to kick her out of the class.'

Erik's reaction when he saw Zina was so pathetic, that it was almost funny. First, he just goggled at her for a bit, and then he went embarrassingly servile, falling over himself to pass her things and making sure she was comfortable. Finally, Bill said in his gravelly voice, 'Well, Zina seems to have stirred things up a bit, at any rate,' and Erik blushed and settled down. All in all, it was a rather uncomfortable class, and Anjali was glad when it was over.

'I'm going in for a shower,' she announced once the door was safely shut behind her students. 'Gayatri, Rhea's mom is sending one of her friends across for the Hindi class. In case she lands up before I'm done, just ask her to wait for a bit and come and tell me, okay?'

'Sure,' Gayatri said. Rhea was one of the girls in her class in school. Gayatri was still adjusting to the school and the way everything was different from her school in Indore, but Rhea and she had hit it off the second they met. Luckily, their mothers got along as well—Rhea's mom was an architect, and she had been very encouraging when Anjali decided to start Hindi classes.

When Anjali came into the room a few minutes later, it was occupied by a pleasantly plump and curvy, very obviously Bengali woman. She was dressed in a rather tight skirt and an even tighter blouse. The blouse was having a tough time keeping her exuberant bosom in check. The whole effect was a bit like Vidya-Balan-in-Dirty-Picture, except for the hair. God had evidently intended it to be curly, but its owner seemed to have subjected it to various straightening techniques before chopping it short with a pair of garden shears.

She had a lovely smile though—warm and infectious, and she turned it on to full-wattage as she bore down on

Anjali. 'I'm so happy to meet you,' she said, and unlike most people, she really seemed to mean it.

'Umm, my daughter took your name down, so I'm not sure I've got it right...Daffodil Banerjee?' Eeks, it sounded even more ridiculous when said out aloud. Anjali found herself crossing her fingers and hoping that the woman didn't snap back and say her name was Debjani or Debasri or something equally normal.

'She got it right,' the woman said, and sighed, running her hand through her short hair and making it stand up even more wildly. 'What can I say, my Dad had literary pretensions.'

'Wordsworth?' Anjali asked, smiling slightly. 'Could have been worse.'

'Blake,' Daffodil said, shuddering eloquently. 'He could have called me "Tiger Tiger". Though I wouldn't have minded Tagore. "Gitanjali".' She sighed and then turned all brisk in a second. 'Anyway, my friends call me "Daffy". Maybe you should call me that as well.'

As far as Anjali was concerned, being called Daffy was just as bad as being called Daffodil. Worse actually, because Daffodil at least didn't sound as if she had stepped out of Looney Toons.

'Right, Daffy,' she said briskly. You're here to enrol for the Hindi class?'

'What else?' The sigh implied that Daffy would rather be getting a root canal done without anaesthetic. 'I did my schooling in Kolkata—Hindi isn't my strong point at all. And in my line of work, it's a handicap if people start thinking "rasogolla" every time I open my mouth.'

'What do you do?' Anjali asked curiously. So far all the people she had met in Mumbai spoke only English at work.

'Market research. And I'm now stuck doing research only for MNC banks and high-end women's products. None of the real FMCG stuff like soaps or detergents...' Realising from Anjali's blank expression that nothing was getting through her head, she laughed. 'Sorry, sorry, I'll explain it all properly some other time. Now, can you fit me in, and when?'

The problem with people with jobs was that they wanted classes on weekends, Anjali had realised. And housewives, unfortunately, didn't seem keen on learning Hindi. Luckily, Sushil worked on most Saturdays, so Saturday mornings were relatively free.

'Saturday morning, nine o'clock!' Daffy sounded positively horrified. 'Can't you make it a little later, like twelve or something?'

'Then it wouldn't be morning any longer,' Anjali pointed out, her lips twitching with suppressed laughter.

Daffodil burst out laughing as well.

'You're right, it wouldn't,' she said. 'How many other students do you have?'

'Just four, apart from you,' Anjali said. 'Three of them are expats. And then there's Zina.'

Daffy's ears pricked up immediately. 'Who's she?

Someone interesting? Your face went all different when you said her name.'

So much for being inscrutable and Sphinx-like. 'She's in training to become a celebrity hairdresser,' Anjali said. 'There's a TV show on makeovers that her boss stars in, and she plans to have a show of her own soon.'

'And you don't like her?'

'What are you, a mind-reader?' Anjali retorted without thinking, and as Daffy turned pink, she held up a hand and said, 'I'm sorry, I didn't mean that. No, I don't like her much, but I can't say it without sounding like a jealous old cow, so I try to pretend that she's like any other student.'

'I've got you another student,' Erik announced a week later. Anjali eyed him with misgiving. 'Another expat?' she asked. Erik's awkwardness had improved with time, but he was still incredibly awkward with the other students. Daffy terrified him with her radical views on everything under the sun, and while he spent a lot of time gazing worshipfully at Zina, he hadn't yet mustered up the courage to hold an actual conversation with her.

'He *is* an expat,' Erik said. 'But he's of Indian descent, or at least his father is. He grew up in Kenya, and he's Mull-yaar-lee, and he's never learnt Hindi.'

'Malayali?' Anjali asked.

Erik nodded in relief. 'Yes, that's it. And he says it's tougher for him than it is for me, because when people see me, they don't *expect* me to know Hindi, but with him they do, and all he knows is a few words. He's quite dark-skinned. Even though his mother's white, he looks very Indian.'

'What a completely racist thing to say,' Daffy remarked to the nearest potted plant, and Erik flushed a brilliant scarlet. 'I didn't mean,' he stammered, but Zina cut him off impatiently. 'Oh don't be silly, Daffy,' she said. 'Ignore her, Erik, she's just being difficult. When's this chap joining the class?'

'Well, er, today, actually,' Erik said looking nervous. 'That's all right, isn't it, Anjali?'

Anil Nair was quite surprisingly good-looking. Erik had been right about his being dark-skinned—he looked as Indian as Zina or Anjali herself, and it was a bit disorienting hearing him struggle over the simplest Hindi sentences. Plus, he had the most atrocious khichdi accent; part-American, part-Kenyan and part 'Mull-yaar-lee'.

'It's also the embarrassment factor, you know,' he said giving Anjali a wry smile. 'I feel like a foreigner in my own country.' 'But can you speak Mull-yaar-lum?' Anjali asked, and then corrected herself hastily. 'Malayalam, I mean.' Damn, Erik's accent was infectious! Anil shook his head mournfully. 'Very little. But I figured that it made more sense learning Hindi given that I'm working in Mumbai. And perhaps Marathi and Gujarati after that.'

He was an ophthalmic surgeon and had decided to move to India after working in the US for several years.

'I didn't quite realise how chaotic Mumbai is, though,' he said, his face creasing into a singularly attractive smile. 'But like my boss in the US used to say, I need to "eat the elephant bite by bite"—Hindi's going to be my first hurdle.'

Anil's joining definitely eased the atmosphere in the class. For one, Anjali was able to split the class into two so that Zina attended the 9 a.m. class with Bill and Lydia, while Erik, Anil and Daffy started at 11. Erik looked a little woebegone when he figured that he'd no longer be in the same class as Zina, but his concentration levels improved dramatically. So did his Hindi, much to Anjali's relief. Sushil had suggested a package pricing deal in which the expats paid an upfront amount, and then a second, much larger sum once they'd actually learnt the language. The system was working well with Bill and Lydia but so far, Erik hadn't gotten beyond 'Dhanyawaad' and 'Shukriya'. Zina and Daffy were on the good old pay-per-class system, and so far, it was working fine.

Hi Ananya!!!

So xcited that ur mom's allowed u 2 hv ur own e-mail id!!!! Wish u were here—miss u like crazy. Mumbai is fun most of the time, but the girls in school are a little mean. I made one gud frnd—Rhea, but still

I want my BFF arnd!!!

How's school and Miss Neelam, Annushka and Kitu? Miss u all!!! Even Princi. Tell ur dad to move here naaa, that wud be so much fun!

Luv,
Gayatri

six

'BUT SHE'S SO dark!' Used to having her fair skin and lovely hair commented favourably upon by all her mother's old friends, Gayatri couldn't understand why her classmates thought the gypsy-ish Alisha Mehta was good-looking. The second she said it though, she realised that she had made a mistake.

'Ooh look, we have a little racist amongst us,' Naina said. 'Remind me again, which part of the United States is Indore in?'

The other girls sniggered and even Rhea looked a little disappointed, as if Gayatri had let her down in some way. Quite suddenly, Gayatri felt like she wanted to cry. Biting down on her lip fiercely to stop the tears, she tossed her head. 'Well anyway, she might be good-looking, but she's really dumb. I heard Miss Vinita tell one of the other teachers that Alisha should have been held back in Standard Four.'

It took less than half the day for that particular remark to get to Alisha, and after that, Gayatri was effectively in Coventry. Except for Rhea and the mousy twins, most of the girls stopped talking to her. Pretending she didn't care, Gayatri started hanging out with the boys instead, wincing at the constant burp-fart-crap jokes. But at least they didn't bother about her clothes or her hair or her accent. And Rhea was still her friend, though she seemed torn between hanging out with a group of girls and being exclusively with Gayatri.

'Dooba, dooba, dooba—Dooobey!' Gayatri made a face. Her surname was a source of endless amusement to her classmates, and Krish Askandani was particularly annoying about it. Probably because he had a weird surname himself, Gayatri decided.

'Guess what?' he said, gurgling with laughter as he came up to her. Krish was a short kid, and he only reached Gayatri's shoulder. 'My aunt's dog swallowed her driver's phone last week.' Gayatri gave Krish a suspicious look. 'And?'

'The driver was too scared to tell her. And every time the dog farted, the phone got pressed against his intestines and called my aunt. And all she could hear when she answered was "burble-gurgle-blub-blub". So when the driver came to pick up the keys yesterday, my aunt asked him, *"Tumhara health mein problem hai kya kuch, har baar bud-bud-bud awaaz karta hai?"'*

'You're such a liar, Krish,' Rhea said, her voice dripping with scorn. 'Why d'you talk to him?' she asked Gayatri as they walked away, leaving Krish laughing happily at his own joke. 'He's a loser.'

Gayatri actually quite liked Krish, but after her recent faux pas, she didn't want to contradict Rhea. 'At least he doesn't stink,' she said, shrugging her shoulders. 'Or talk about football all the time.'

'Hmm, right,' Rhea said. Then she perked up. 'You all set for the weekend? I packed last night. My mom's bringing my bag to school when she comes to pick me up. We'll go for lunch, and then we'll meet you guys at Bhiwandi before we drive to the farm.' Their families had booked a weekend at a nearby farm, and both the girls were excited.

'My mom packed for me,' Gayatri said, and Rhea rolled her eyes. 'Yes, clothes and shoes, of course. I meant the stuff for midnight snacks and games and all of that.'

'My mom packed those as well,' Gayatri said. There was no point fibbing to Rhea—she always figured things out. 'But most of it is stuff I told her to put in.' She gave Rhea a wistful look. Anjali never took Gayatri out for lunch, and she'd have to take the school bus home and eat boring daal-chawal before they left for the farm.

The weekend plan had been a last minute thing arranged by Anjali and Rhea's mother, Devika. Rhea had been invited for a sleepover that Devika didn't want her to go for. Gayatri hadn't been invited, and it seemed like the perfect opportunity to wean Rhea away from a bunch of girls whom Devika deeply disliked.

'What does the husband do?' Sushil asked as they left home—complete with two suitcases and a hyper daughter.

'Gautam? He owns a sporting goods company. And Devika's an architect.'

'I know, she told me the last time we met,' Sushil said. 'Sounded like she's got a bit of a chip on her shoulder about people assuming she's a housewife.'

'It's not a chip exactly,' Anjali said, hoping Sushil wouldn't take it upon himself to bait Devika through the weekend. He had largely grown out of his contrarian phase, but sometimes it resurfaced with a vengeance. If he didn't find Gautam entertaining company, it was very likely he'd create his own entertainment by needling Devika into losing her temper.

'Have you called the driver?' she asked him once they reached the ground floor.

Sushil frowned. 'I tried his phone a few times, but I couldn't get through to him. Let's walk to the parking lot.' The driver was a relatively new hire, and Anjali was still in two minds about him. On the plus side, he was from UP and spoke excellent Hindi. In fact, he was the only person Anjali had met so far in Mumbai who was capable of holding a grammatically correct conversation in the language. On the minus side, he was cross-eyed and built on the lines of an army tank—but as Sushil had pointed out correctly, being cross-eyed didn't matter much because while he was driving you had to look at only one side of his face.

What tilted the scales against Tiwari was an airy confession of having a charge pending against him at the local police station. When Anjali asked him what the charge was, he told her that he had assaulted a 'pandu' for abusing him at a traffic signal. Clearly he thought that such behaviour was well within his rights as a citizen of a free country—he was deeply resentful of having to go to court to fight the case every few weeks.

Right now, there was no sign of Tiwari in the parking lot, though the car was in its usual spot. On closer examination, Sushil noticed that the front seat was reclined to the maximum possible setting, and a head of tousled hair was visible from the window.

'He's asleep!' Sushil said incredulously, knocking on the door of the car. Tiwari didn't seem to hear it, because they could see him snuggle into a more comfortable position on the seat.

'Maybe we should just leave him there and take a cab?' Anjali suggested. 'We could meet up with Devika and Gautam somewhere and go in their car.' Sushil stared at her as if she had lost her mind.

'While he stinks up my car snoring away in it? And how do we know what he'll do with the car once he finally wakes up?'

He gave the window another peremptory rap and

the driver sat up, giving them a wild-eyed stare before collapsing back on the seat.

'He's drunk,' Sushil said, flushing up in anger. Anjali was more charitable. 'Perhaps he just has a hangover?' she suggested.

'What's a hangover?' Gayatri enquired. Sushil turned abruptly. 'Anjali, take Gayatri, and go and stand in the lobby,' he ordered, and Anjali went.

Sushil banged on the door once more, loud enough this time for two security guards to come to the car. Tiwari finally woke up, and rolled the window down to look blearily at Sushil and the guards.

'*Gaadi ke baahar aao,*' Sushil said sharply. Tiwari gave him an obedient nod, turned over and went back to sleep. One of the guards leaned into the car and shook him by the shoulder.

'*Sahib kab se bulaa rahein hain, utho!*' he said, and finally something seemed to seep through Tiwari's befuddled brain. He staggered out of the car, and Sushil got into the driver's seat without giving Tiwari a second glance.

'Thanks,' he said curtly to the guards. 'Just see that he washes his face and goes home, will you? I don't want him wandering around the complex in this condition.'

He drove to the lobby, while Tiwari looked after him with a rather hurt expression on his face. 'Will he be okay?' Anjali asked as she got into the car.

'I don't f...really care,' Sushil said, suppressing the expletive because of Gayatri's presence. 'I'll sack him the day we get back.'

Ironically, Anjali found herself wanting to defend Tiwari. Poor man, he had a tough life living alone in Mumbai, so what if he landed up at work with a hangover once in a while? A quick glance at Sushil's rigid profile made her decide to save the discussion for later—he looked like he was about to explode with anger.

It was after a good fifteen minutes of driving that Sushil finally relaxed. 'Where are we meeting the Deshpandes?' he asked.

'Bhiwandi,' Anjali said, consulting the printout on her lap. 'After that we need to take the Nasik road for a bit and then turn towards Vikramgadh.'

'Sounds very Sholay-like,' Sushil commented, swinging the car onto the Eastern Express Highway. He enjoyed driving and, in a way, he didn't regret that the original plan of Tiwari driving them up to Thane hadn't worked out. His phone beeped and he told Anjali, 'Could you check that please? I was expecting a message from my HDFC Relationship Manager.'

Anjali picked up the phone and burst out laughing. 'It's from Tiwari,' she said, reading out the message. '"Bhaiyya, very sorry". Should I reply?'

'Let him stew a bit,' Sushil said, but he was smiling as well.

Tiwari was clearly going into a frenzy of remorse, because the second and third message came in within the next few seconds.

'*Bhabhi ko bhi sorry,*' the second one said, and the third said, '*Phir kabhi nahin hoga.*'

'I'm telling him it's fine,' Anjali said, taking the phone and typing out 'Okay'. 'Otherwise he might come after us to apologise in person.'

'Can we put some music on?' Gayatri said impatiently. 'I'm tired of Tiwari and his messages.' Anjali reached across and slid a CD into the car's music system. Gone were the days when she could listen to Bollywood oldies peacefully in the car. A taste for Western music was one of the first things Gayatri had picked up from her friends, and the entire family was now forced to listen to girl bands all the time.

Somehow, Anjali had expected Bhiwandi to be a pretty town—its stark ugliness was a shock. One hideous building was followed by another, and all of them had the corrugated iron roofs and rolling shutters so beloved to small-town builders.

'You can't expect it to look nice just because it sounds a bit like Bhopal,' Sushil said.

'I expected it to look nice because it's a small town,' Anjali said sadly. 'But this is even worse than Mumbai. I don't think I want to stop here for chai after all. Let me check with Devika on how far they've reached—we can wait for them at the beginning of the highway.'

Luckily Gautam and Devika were only a few minutes behind them, and Sushil let their glossy Audi overtake before he swung his Honda CRV back onto the road. 'Devika's driving, is she?' he asked, and Anjali gave him an apprehensive look. Sushil had distilled every piece of MCP training he got in his growing up years into a firm aversion for women drivers. Women CEOs were okay, as were women politicians and astronauts, but as far as driving went, he thought Saudi Arabia was the only country with a sensible policy on the subject.

'She's not bad,' he said grudgingly after a bit, and Anjali heaved a sigh of relief. Perhaps the weekend wasn't going to be that bad after all.

'There's a frog in the sink!'

'Chase it out then,' Gayatri yelled back. 'But hurry up, I need to use the loo.' There was a second's silence, then a little scream. 'Yeuch, it's *jumping* at me!'

Gayatri groaned. 'It's a *frog*,' she said. 'That's what frogs *do*! Now will you hurry up and finish brushing your teeth or putting on your lip gloss or whatever it is you're doing in there.'

The door opened suddenly and Rhea shot out, looking several shades paler than normal. 'It's all yours,' she said. 'I'm going to my mom's room and using the loo there.'

Gayatri stuck her head around the door. The frog was small and yellow, and was looking at her with the loveliest golden eyes. 'It's beautiful,' she said involuntarily, and Rhea snorted. 'Give it a smooch then,' she said. 'Maybe it'll turn into Justin Bieber. I'm out of here.'

The farm had been booked by Devika, and while the surroundings were lovely, the accommodation was pretty basic. Apparently Devika was going through a phase in which she decided to bring her family 'closer to nature'—with the family kicking and screaming all the way. Rhea's older sister had wisely opted out of the trip and gone to stay with her grandparents for the weekend. Gayatri herself loved the farm and the rustic feel of the place, but Rhea had taken one look at the place and decided that she'd much rather be at the sleepover that she had been invited for. Since then, she had been whiny and out of sorts with Gayatri.

Five minutes later, Rhea was back, looking completely grossed out. Gayatri gave her an inquiring look.

'Aren't they in the room?'

'They are,' Rhea muttered, getting into bed and turning her back to Gayatri. 'They were *making out*! That's why they sent us off to our room—and they're so old—yuck, it's disgusting!'

Gayatri didn't think it was disgusting. Her own parents had gotten back together only a few months ago, and she was secretly thrilled by any display of affection between the two of them. But that wasn't something she could talk about. They'd never told her to say it, but she always pretended that her parents had a perfectly normal relationship. It wasn't even difficult—Sushil had been around during her holidays, and she had enough anecdotes about things they'd done together when she was younger.

Rhea was still frowning, and Gayatri asked tentatively, 'Did you get to use the loo?' For a second, she thought Rhea was going to flip out completely, but then she caught her eye, and they both burst into helpless giggles.

'No, I didn't,' Rhea said finally. 'Is the frog still there?'

It wasn't, but Rhea insisted on Gayatri standing guard just outside the bathroom, ready to rush in to the rescue if the frog reappeared. Later, when they were both in bed, Gayatri asked drowsily, 'Did you see my parents? They said they were going for a walk.'

Rhea hesitated. She *had* seen Gayatri's parents, but did not mention it on purpose because it looked like they were having a fight.

'I thought I saw them,' she said finally. 'But they were a long way off.' She bounced up and picked up her iPad and held it in front of her stomach with the screen facing outwards. 'Look, I'm a Teletubby!'

Gayatri gave her a blank look. 'What's a Teletubby?' This kept happening—Rhea would use a word or a phrase that Gayatri didn't recognise, and then laugh or get impatient when she asked for an explanation. This time though, Rhea just looked disgusted. 'Why do I even bother,' she muttered, flopping back against her pillow and turning her back to Gayatri.

From Rhea's perspective, this was the ultimate weekend from hell. Missing the sleepover meant that her last chance of joining the Golden Girls Gang was gone. She didn't like the four girls who made up the group as much as she liked Gayatri, but she was flattered when they'd started taking notice of her.

'So, what is a Tellytubby?' Gayatri asked, feeling uncharacteristically pugnacious. 'Someone with an iPad growing out of her tummy?'

'A television screen,' Rhea said morosely. 'You'd have known what it was if you hadn't spent your life stuck in a village.'

In the next cottage, Anjali was still looking distinctly upset and Sushil sighed and pulled her into his arms. 'I'm sorry,' he said against her hair. 'I was just trying to be friendly with her, because she's such a good friend of yours.'

The whole thing had started because of a completely innocuous remark that Devika had made about single mothers and their Tiger Mom tendencies. Sushil's response had been flippant, and he hadn't noticed Anjali tense up and fall silent. She had not told Devika about the years she lived apart from Sushil because it had been simpler not to—there was no way Devika could have known she was treading on Anjali's toes with every remark she made. Sushil was another matter. Either he was being deliberately insensitive, or he was just plain dumb. At that time, she thought he was being insensitive, and she had sat through the evening feeling more and more upset as he laughed and joked with the Deshpandes and completely ignored her. Now, however, she was inclining towards the 'plain dumb' theory.

'I'm not jealous,' she explained slowly and patiently. 'I'm just upset because you're an insensitive git.'

'Git' was Gayatri's favourite word, picked up from the Harry Potter books, and Anjali had adopted it with relief. She didn't feel comfortable at all with the f-word, or even with mild swearing—she had been shocked by the language used even by Devika and Gautam when the kids weren't around. Unfortunately, 'bewakoof' and 'gadhaa' didn't have the cachet of a proper English swear word, and she had started using 'git' as a substitute.

'Because I said single moms think the sun shines out of their kids' backsides? Come on, I just said it because it sounded funny!'

'It didn't,' Anjali said, sighing and putting her head on Sushil's comfortingly solid chest. 'Can we go to bed now? I'm sick of arguing.'

Sushil immediately brightened up. 'Bed' was a word he understood and knew what to do with. And thankfully, Devika had booked a separate cottage for the kids, which meant he didn't have to bother about Gayatri popping in at an awkward moment.

It took Anjali half of the next day to realise that Gayatri and Rhea were no longer talking to each other. Both families had gone for a trek to a nearby waterfall, and in the climbing and subsequent splashing around, it hadn't registered that each girl was sticking to her own parents. It was only during lunch that she noticed that the normal chatter between them was missing.

'Have you had a fight with Rhea?' she asked Gayatri quietly when the girl went to wash her hands. Everyone else was still finishing dessert, but Gayatri still gave the table a quick glance before shaking her head. 'Why isn't she talking to you then?' Anjali persisted.

'She is. Don't fuss, Mom,' Gayatri said, but Anjali wasn't able to leave it alone. Gayatri didn't talk much about school, but Anjali couldn't help feeling that things weren't okay. Her grades were excellent, even in subjects like French and Marathi which she was doing for the first time. But except for Rhea and some of the boys who took the same bus, she didn't seem to have many friends. She was invited for birthday parties, but not for sleepovers, and the other girls from her class called only when they needed help with homework.

'Devika, do you know if the girls have had a fight?' Devika bit her lip. 'Yes, I think something happened,' she said. 'Ignore it Anjali, it's best if they patch it up on their own.' So Anjali did her best to ignore it and by the end of the day, the girls were talking again.

They had one more night at the farm, and they spent the evening around a bonfire singing old songs, accompanied by Gautam on an old guitar he had borrowed from the owner of the farm. Some of the other guests joined in as well, and they continued singing past dinner. Around ten, both the girls fell asleep, and their dads carried them back to their room.

'They've made up, haven't they?' Devika asked and Anjali nodded though she still felt a little uneasy about the vibes between the kids. It was unlike them to hang out with the adults—she expected them to go back to their room and giggle and gossip. But if Devika hadn't picked up on it, maybe she was imagining things.

'I don't think they liked the farm much,' she said instead. 'Bit of a waste of money, wasn't it? Twenty thousand for two nights. It's almost as much as what you'd pay to rent a flat, isn't it?'

'Not really,' Devika said. 'You guys must be paying upwards of two lakhs a month for your place.'

'No, of course not…' Anjali started to say, then she pulled up short as she realised that she really didn't know how much rent Sushil was paying for their flat. But two lakhs sounded really exorbitant—surely he wasn't shelling out that much? She asked him when they were alone together, and he laughed. 'My company pays,' he said. 'Part of the rent's adjusted against the deposit, and I get a tax deduction—it isn't as extravagant as it sounds.' Anjali nodded, though she wasn't convinced. Two lakhs was two lakhs, whichever way you looked at it. Sushil currently managed his money without discussing it with her—he was more than generous when it came to household expenses, and for the first time, Anjali wondered whether he was *too* generous. Was he saving any money at all? Perhaps when they got home she'd ask him if he had set up a college fund for Gayatri. And whether they should consider buying a flat rather than renting one.

'Did you have a good time?' Sushil asked Gayatri as they drove back. 'Not really,' Gayatri said. 'The place sucks.'

'Gayatri!' Anjali said sharply. Sushil was still settling into being a 365-days-a-year dad, and sometimes he over-reacted when he thought Gayatri was being cheeky—it was always better to head Gayatri off before they had an altercation. Gayatri shrugged and put on a pair of headphones as she buried her face in a Percy Jackson book, effectively shutting out her parents. Anjali sighed. At times, she felt like she wasn't equipped to be a 365-days-a-year parent either.

'I need a new pair of football studs,' Gayatri said suddenly as they neared home. 'Mine tore on Thursday. Can we stop and buy them now?' Wellington had a strong girls' football team, and Gayatri had just managed to scrape into it the previous week. Anjali suspected that this was because two of the better players had suddenly developed a lady-like aversion to the game, but she hadn't wanted to dampen Gayatri's enthusiasm.

Sushil looked at his watch and said, 'Not now. I've booked the tennis court for 6.00, and we won't reach in time if we go to a mall. Pick them up during the week.'

'But I have a match tomorrow!' Gayatri was beginning to look upset, and Anjali jumped into the breach. 'Why don't you drop us off at Palladium?' she suggested. 'I have a couple of other things to pick up as well, and we can take a cab back.'

It was like negotiating an arms treaty, Anjali thought wearily after Sushil dropped them off. Nowadays everything seemed to turn into a yelling match between Sushil and Gayatri, and in all fairness she couldn't blame Sushil. Gayatri was going through a bad phase, and according to Devika who had an older daughter, it was likely to get a lot worse when she entered her teens.

'Look, there's Zina!' Gayatri said, pointing towards a jewellery store. Anjali followed her gaze. There she was indeed, looking over a rack of clothes with a man around her own height. Anjali was about to tell Gayatri that they probably shouldn't disturb her when Zina turned around and saw them.

'Hi!' Gayatri said, raising an arm and waving, and both Anjali and Zina cursed under their breath in the same instant. Zina liked Gayatri, but right at this moment, she couldn't be bothered with a little girl. Her birthday was coming up, and Ishaan had decided with characteristic suddenness that he wanted to get her a pair of earrings. She was having a lovely time looking at every set of earrings in the store—there were simple gold hoops and long chandelier earrings dripping with diamonds, and a funky pair of studs in rose gold that she really liked. She had no idea what Ishaan's budget was, and the studs were one of the less expensive pairs in the store. Even then, they cost upwards of thirty thousand, and her usually dormant conscience was pricking her.

Gayatri was already in the store, and Zina turned to smile at her. 'Hey little pumpkin,' she said, giving her a casual pat on the cheek. 'Buying Mommy some diamonds?'

'No,' Gayatri giggled. 'That's Dad's job. I needed football shoes. Are you buying those?' She leaned over to peer at the studs. 'They're so pretty. My friend has a pair just like them.'

Except that the stones in her friend's earrings were probably glass, Zina thought, giving the earrings a last wistful glance. 'No, I'm not,' she said. 'Ishaan, on second thoughts, I'd like a voucher for the Thai spa on the third floor. I'll only end up losing the earrings.'

Anjali came up in time to hear the last sentence, and Zina could see the surprise in her eyes. Clearly she had thought that Zina would milk a man for everything she could get out of him.

'Anjali, meet Ishaan,' she said, pulling Ishaan forward and wishing that he didn't look quite so young. Not that she cared about Anjali's opinion, but she was used to people seeing her with a man and thinking, 'What does she see in him?' This was the first time that there was a risk of the question being flipped.

Ishaan held out a hand, and Anjali took it, giving him a polite smile. There was something terribly familiar about the boy, but she couldn't place him. Mentally she ran through the places she could have met him before. He didn't look old enough to be a colleague of Sushil's, and he wasn't a neighbour either. God knows where Zina had found him—she first thought he was one of the trainees in Rehaan's salon, but now that she looked at him closely, she realised that he was way too well-dressed to be a trainee hairdresser.

Impulsively, she asked, 'Have we met before? I'm sure I've seen you somewhere.'

'Maybe you saw me at a restaurant or something,' he said. 'I don't think we've been introduced—I'd definitely have remembered you.'

The compliment was as well-phrased as it was subtle, but Anjali had had too many years of experience dealing with admiring undergrads. 'Thank you,' she said solemnly. 'But I have a pretty terrible memory, so if I recognise you it's likely to be either because I actually met you, or because I've mixed you up with someone else.'

Gayatri turned around at the sound of his laugh and looked at Ishaan carefully for the first time. 'Hi,' she said, her eyes turning wary. 'You're Alisha's older brother, aren't you? You'd come for our Annual Day.'

Alisha Mehta was Gayatri's sixteen-year-old nemesis, the senior she had offended with her stupid remarks—first about her looks and then, her brains. Alisha hadn't deigned to even acknowledge her existence, but she had made sure Gayatri was out of the running as far as popularity stakes went.

'Ah, so that's where I saw you,' Anjali said. Her manner had changed, Zina noticed—two minutes back, she was mildly flirting with Ishaan, and now she sounded like she was his aunt. 'So you're Dr Suhasini Mehta's son?'

Ishaan nodded, his eyes sparkling with mischief. 'Don't tell me, she's been calling you for that fund-raiser of hers.'

'Actually, yes, she has,' Anjali admitted. 'But she's pretty well-known otherwise as well. And Alisha is Gayatri's house captain, isn't that right?'

Gayatri nodded, biting her lip. Her mother didn't know about the problems at school, and as far as she was concerned, Alisha was just another senior.

Ishaan caught the look on Gayatri's face, and said, 'Alisha can be a bit of a bully at times—don't let her boss you around, okay?' He gave her a quick smile, and Gayatri blushed in confusion. So far, she hadn't really noticed the opposite sex much, or not real boys at least, only movie stars and teen singing sensations. Ishaan's striking looks were having an effect on her though, and she kept gazing at him even after his attention was distracted by the shopkeeper.

'See you at class tomorrow then,' Anjali said to Zina. She was holding a class on Monday for Zina and Lydia to make up for the Saturday class that she cancelled. Zina nodded, and Anjali pulled Gayatri out of the store, as disturbed by her staring at Ishaan as Zina was.

Zina sank her face into her hands. 'I'm such a cradle-snatcher,' she groaned. 'Oh God, Ishaan—d'you realise, that *baby* fancies you. How old is she? Ten?'

'Around twelve I think,' Ishaan said, trying not to

laugh. 'Relax Zina, she probably fancies Brad Pitt as well, that doesn't make Angelina Jolie a cradle-snatcher, does it?'

'I don't know,' Zina said. Grabbing Ishaan's arm, she hustled him out of the store. 'Ishaan, this can't go on. You're just too damn *young* for me!'

'Really?' Ishaan said, and put a firm hand under her chin, tipping her face up just a bit so that she was forced to look at him. His eyes were glinting with mischief and suppressed desire, and Zina felt her knees go weak with longing. So *what* if he was years younger than her? It wasn't like she was planning to marry him and have his babies—this was supposed to be for pure fun.

'My mom's out of town,' Ishaan said softly. 'And Alisha's at a friend's place. Want to come over?'

'I didn't even know you had a sister,' Zina said weakly, allowing herself to be led out of the mall and towards the parking lot. Ishaan shrugged. 'It isn't important,' he said, opening the car door for her. 'I also have two aunts and a Labrador—I'm sure you don't want to hear about them, do you?'

'I don't like dogs,' Zina managed, and Ishaan leaned across the gear shift and kissed her on the lips.

'Ah, finally something you're scared of,' he said mockingly. 'Don't worry, Tughlaq is with my mom in Alibagh.'

Much later, when they were in bed together in his mother's massive South Mumbai flat, Ishaan reached across and pulled something out of the pocket of his discarded jeans. 'Here,' he said, 'Happy birthday in advance.'

Zina stared at the diamond studs in surprise. 'But when?' she stuttered. 'I thought I told you not to get them!'

Ishaan gave her a lazy smile. 'I liked the way they looked on you,' he said. 'Put them on.' His voice was huskily compelling, and she found herself taking off her cheap silver earrings and sliding the white gold ones in. She could see her reflection in the mirror opposite the bed—tousled hair, and bare shoulders showing above the sheet she had pulled up to cover her breasts. The earrings glinted in her ears, and she admired them for a second before giving Ishaan a troubled look.

'I don't think I should accept these,' she said. If his mother found out that he was spending her hard-earned money buying gifts for his much-older girlfriend, she'd probably come after Zina with a knife. He gave her a deliberately puzzled look. 'What's the matter, don't like them anymore?'

The problem was that she loved them, and he knew it. 'It's not right,' she tried to explain, though her subconscious was telling her scornfully to shut up and keep the damn earrings. 'You shouldn't be spending your mother's money on me.'

'You're right, I shouldn't,' Ishaan said, nodding seriously. Damn, now she'd have to give the earrings back. Served her right for developing a conscience so late in life. 'Would it help if I told you it's not her money?'

Zina stared at him. 'Whose is it then?'

'Mine,' Ishaan said easily. 'My father was stinking rich, and he left me a pot of money. And I'm pretty good at playing the stock market. I make more than enough to pay for my expensive tastes.'

Presumably she was one of the expensive tastes, but the smile he gave her robbed the words of their sting. 'Doesn't your mom have a say in how you spend the money?'

Ishaan shook his head. 'Their marriage was pretty much on the rocks when my dad did her a favour and died of a heart attack.'

Registering Zina's shocked expression, he said, 'He was a pretty terrible husband. Decent dad though.'

'D'you miss him?' Zina asked tentatively. 'Used to,' Ishaan said with a shrug and held out his arms. 'Come here,' he said, and she collapsed back into his arms. 'I can't handle too much heavy conversation at one go,' he said, nibbling seductively at her earlobe. 'We'll talk about my complicated family some other time, okay?'

'Right,' she managed to gasp as his mouth and hands reduced her limbs to jelly. It felt so good—and he was right, who wanted to talk about boring parents when they could be doing something a lot more fun?

※

Dear Nanaji,

Can I come to Indore for Diwali? Am missing you a lot.

Love,
Gayatri

seven

'I SEE A woman's dress in his cupboard, and it is really horrible, green like a snake's skin, and I think—ha, he is having an affair! Finally I catch him!'

Lydia paused for dramatic effect, and Anjali asked, 'Was he?'

Lydia shook her head vehemently. '*Nyet*, that is where I am wrong!!! Never have I thought to see such a thing.' She leaned forward, and put a hand on Anjali's knee and whispered, 'You will never tell anyone?'

'I won't,' Anjali said, wondering what was coming next. Over time, Anjali had found herself becoming a sort of agony aunt for Lydia and Daffy and even for Erik—she had always been a good listener, and after every class, one or the other of them hung around to tell her about their latest woes.

'The dress is *his*!!!' Lydia said and slapped her slim thighs in a surprisingly mannish gesture. '*He* is wearing it, when no one is at home, and is looking at himself in the mirror. So I say, at least if you have to wear woman's dress, wear a good one!!! Not cheap department store what do you say—knock-off.' 'Was he upset that you found out?' Anjali was trying desperately to dispel a mental image of Lydia's husband dressed in a slinky green dress—it was all very well for Lydia to laugh at him, but she'd probably be mortally offended if Anjali did the same. Lydia snorted. 'Scared,' she said succinctly. 'And also, how do you say? Embarrassed. Because I tell him the dress is not good.'

'Perhaps you could, umm, help him choose a better brand next time,' Anjali said, and winced at how it ended up sounding. Way to go Anjali, plan a joint girls shopping trip with him, why don't you? Lydia thankfully didn't seem at all offended.

'That is good idea,' she said, frowning slightly. 'Only am not sure, I think men's clothes better for him. Why women's clothes?'

Feeling completely not up to explaining the psychology of a transvestite, Anjali shook her head in regret. 'I don't know,' she said. 'But it's not like a mental health problem or anything, perhaps you just need to accept him the way he is.'

'It hadn't even occurred to her that it might be a mental health issue,' she told Sushil after Lydia left. 'Me and my big mouth. Before you know it, she'll have poor Kumar fitted for a straightjacket.'

Sushil roared with laughter. 'Not she,' he said. 'Kumar

makes more money in a month than most of us do in a year—there's no way she's going to risk *that* drying up. So what if he likes wearing Victoria's Secret once in a while? That's his and Lydia's secret.' He looked at Anjali's arrested expression and said, 'Stop looking so scandalised,' he said. 'Money is a big factor for many women.'

'Women like me?' Anjali asked in a low voice. She was nowhere near pulling any kind of financial weight, and Sushil still pretty much paid for everything.

'Women like you throw their husbands out if they don't behave,' Sushil said, a smile tugging at the corners of his mouth. 'And maybe I'm flattering myself, but I do think that I'm more bearable than a bald cross-dresser with a beer belly.'

'Thanks,' Anjali said. 'Go away now, my next batch of students is about to land up.'

'I don't think he values me enough,' Daffy said thoughtfully, lingering at the door after the class was over and Erik had left.

'Your boyfriend?'

Daffy nodded. 'He says he's totally supportive of my career, but he keeps making stupid little digs at Market Research—the other day he told me that research is the most expensive piece of toilet paper a marketeer can use to cover his ass. Which is funny in its own way, but it's not particularly nice to hear.'

Anjali nodded in what she hoped was a suitably

sympathetic manner. She had never met Daffy's boyfriend, but from what she heard of him, he sounded perfectly obnoxious.

'And there's also the culture thing,' Daffy said sadly. 'He doesn't like reading or classical music, and I totally respect that.' Like all self-respecting Bengalis, Daffy was big on literature and Rabindrasangeet, and the strain of having a Punjabi boyfriend who liked Archie comics and *bhangra* was beginning to show. 'But he keeps making fun of the books I read, and that isn't on? And the other day, he said he hoped I didn't cook in *sarson ka tel* because he hates the smell.' Her nostrils quivered in annoyance. 'Even my mom doesn't use mustard oil, it's always been sunflower oil, and I don't know why he said it, unless he was just trying to rile me up...' She chewed her lip for a bit, and asked Anjali suddenly, 'D'you think I should chuck him?'

'It's your decision,' Anjali said in surprise. 'It doesn't matter what I think. I've never even met Suren.'

'I know it's my decision, but what do *you* think?' Daffy urged her. 'Most of my friends say I'm mad, getting worked up about small things.'

Anjali hesitated. 'I don't think you're mad,' she said finally. 'You remind me of this girl I went to college with. Her boyfriend was a bit like yours, always trying to put her down. She married him, but they split up last year. It's a bit messy because they have a kid.'

'I'll chuck him,' Daffy said firmly. 'There's no way

I'm going to end up like that friend of yours. Thanks Anjali!' Anjali was just about to disclaim all responsibility for Daffy dumping her boyfriend when someone knocked on the door. 'I forgot my iPad,' Erik said, looking a bit shamefaced. 'Ah, there it is, behind that chair.' He hesitated a little, and Daffy gave him a suspicious look. 'Did you forget it on purpose?' she demanded. 'If there's something you need to talk to Anjali about, I'll clear out.'

Erik blushed a vivid shade of red. 'No-ooo,' he stammered. 'I mean, there is a small thing I needed to ask her advice on, but you don't need to go.' 'Is it about Jayanti?' Anjali asked gently, and Erik nodded in relief. 'It is,' he said. 'I want her to leave, but she's refusing to take a hint and I'm worried she'll make a fuss if I sack her.'

'Jayanti's his helper,' Anjali explained. She had figured some time ago that 'servant' or 'maid' weren't acceptable terms, at least not for Erik.

'Can't you just tell her to go because you've found someone else?' Daffy asked. Erik shook his head. 'I haven't, that's the problem,' he said gloomily. 'And Jayanti sits around the whole day and does sweet nothing, other than watching TV and making phone-calls.'

'D'you want me to come and talk to her?' Anjali asked. 'One of my helpers was going that way, and I managed to sort her out pretty quick.'

'If you could,' Erik said gratefully. 'I'm not able to get through to her, somehow—it's like she doesn't understand what I'm telling her.'

'Anjali's turning into a proper problem-solver,' Daffy said with a quick smile. 'She just figured something out for me, and now she's going to manage Jayanti for you.'

'She's a bit like Miss Marple I think,' Erik said. 'She has all this experience from living in a small city, and now she's in Mumbai, she uses her understanding of people to draw a "village parallel". Only instead of murders she solves domestic problems.'

'You read Agatha Christie?' Daffy looked a little surprised, and Erik flushed.

'There's a library near my house, and the only books they had worth reading are the Agatha Christies.'

'Oh, I love Miss Marple,' Daffy said, picking up her huge handbag and heading towards the door. 'Much better than Poirot, don't you think? By the way, if your local library isn't that good, I'll give you the link to an online library—you can select the books you want online, and they'll drop them home for you.'

'I'd definitely be interested,' Erik said, following Daffy out. 'Thanks Anjali, I'll see you next week,' he said, giving her a shy smile. Anjali smiled back. Without Zina to distract him, Erik had become a lot more confident and outgoing—or at least, he was no longer terrified of Daffy. As she went to latch the door she could hear them discussing Ruth Rendell and P. D. James in the corridor, and Erik sounded perfectly sensible and not boring in the least.

Once they'd gone, Anjali called Anil Nair. He had missed

his second class in a row—the first time he let her know but this time he hadn't even texted.

He picked up on the second ring. 'Hi,' he said. 'I'm so sorry, I've not been well. I meant to come today, but I took some really strong cough medicine last night, and it completely knocked me out. I didn't even hear the alarm.'

His voice was barely a croak, and Anjali said, 'No worries, I'll do a couple of separate classes for you later so that you catch up with the rest.'

'That would be great,' he said. 'I'll call you and fix a time soon, okay?'

'Yes of course,' she said. 'Just make sure you've got your voice back first though.' She was smiling when she put the phone down. Over the last few weeks, she found herself getting very fond of Anil. He had a dry sense of humour and unusually for a man, he was an excellent listener. He was the only one amongst Anjali's students whom she had confided in about the difficulties she had had adjusting to Mumbai, and he had been sympathetic without being condescending. So while the rest of her students seemed to assume that agony aunt services came free with Hindi coaching, Anil was the person Anjali turned to when she was feeling low.

'Mom, I really don't want to do Kathak anymore,' Gayatri said three days later. Anjali sighed. Gayatri had been learning Kathak in Indore, and she was pretty good. She'd whine about it even then because the rest of her friends were learning Bollywood dancing Shiamak Davar style, but she'd been obedient enough to put on her ghungroos and go for her classes whenever Anjali told her to. Now, in her newly rebellious phase, she had decided that the new Kathak teacher Anjali had found for her was 'boring'. What she really wanted to learn was ballet, only she was a little too old to start now.

'Look, I've let you take every other class you wanted to,' Anjali said. 'Humour me on this one.' Gayatri was taking swimming and gymnastics lessons and also learning to play the guitar—in Anjali's personal opinion, she'd do a lot better focussing on her studies exclusively. But exactly like she had in Indore, she bowed to peer pressure, only wincing a little at how much more expensive the classes were.

'I'll go today, but I'll stop from next week,' Gayatri bargained, and Anjali lost her temper. 'If you stop Kathak, you can stop all other classes as well,' she said firmly. 'And we can forget about that iPod for your birthday.'

'Papa'll get me the iPod even if you don't,' Gayatri muttered, and Anjali felt like slapping her. And Sushil while she was in the flow of things. He appropriated the 'good cop' role for himself as far as their daughter was concerned, leaving Anjali to be the far less glamorous bad cop.

'Tiwariji, chaliye,' Anjali told the driver shortly. She didn't want to reprimand Gayatri in front of the driver, but she made a mental note to have a serious chat with her in the evening.

After dropping Gayatri off at her class in Breach Candy, Anjali took herself off to stock up on birthday gifts at the Crossword store at Kemps Corner. Every week there was some birthday party or the other—in the beginning, Anjali had tried to choose personalised gifts—after a couple of months she had given up and resorted to buying gifts in bulk and dispensing them in random order. Gayatri's class was an hour long, and gave her enough time to run chores in the area.

'You're a serious Rick Riordan fan I see,' an amused voice said next to her, and Anjali looked up to see Anil Nair smiling down at her.

'Oh, hi', she said. 'Actually, I do like Rick Riordan, but these are for Gayatri's friends. Your voice sounds a lot better now.'

'I'll be back to work tomorrow,' he said. 'Giving myself an extra day because I didn't want to pass on something nasty to my patients.'

'Considerate of you,' Anjali said. 'Here, help me hold these while I try to locate my debit card.'

Once she had paid, Anil said, 'Would you like to have coffee? Unless you're in a hurry?'

'If you promise to talk only in Hindi,' Anjali warned him. 'You're hopelessly out of practice going by what you said to the security guard.'

Anil winced. 'Don't remind me.' The security guard had stared at him as if he was speaking in Swahili when he tried to ask him where the gift wrapping counter was.

'I won't be able to come for this Saturday's class either,' Anil said. 'I've had to reschedule some patients to Saturday morning.'

Anjali was conscious of a little pang of disappointment.

'Some other day in the week?'

'Thursday afternoons are usually good,' he said. 'I don't have surgery then.'

Anjali sighed. 'Thursday is Gayatri's gym class,' she said.

'Surely she doesn't need you to ferry her around?'

'I'm not comfortable leaving her alone with the driver. And...' she hesitated a little. 'I might be a little selfish, but she's already beginning to outgrow me—I want to spend whatever time I can with her.'

'You're not being selfish,' Anil said softly. 'What time is this class? Maybe we can still work something out.'

'5.00 to 6.00,' Anjali said glumly. 'There isn't time for me to get from Peddar Road to Mahalakshmi and back again.'

'I have an idea,' Anil said, hesitating a little. 'If you're okay with it, why don't we have the class at my flat? It's on Peddar Road, and it has a nice balcony that would be perfect for Hindi conversation lessons. And I make a pretty good cup of filter coffee.'

'Yes, sure,' Anjali said, not giving herself time to think. She had picked up on the hesitation, and the implicit acknowledgement of the attraction between them. Also the implicit understanding that they wouldn't do anything about it. Anil didn't know anything of Anjali and Sushil's history—he assumed they were a happily married couple like any other, and Anjali didn't plan to enlighten him. Right now, her number one priority was her daughter and while her marriage wasn't perfect, she was reasonably happy in it.

'We'll start the day after tomorrow then?' Anil asked, and Anjali nodded.

On the day of the actual class though, Anjali began to feel a bit nervous. She had led a fairly sheltered life, and had never visited a bachelor's home before. Unconsciously, she expected the flat to be a mess with ashtrays and old magazines littering the living room. Finding herself in a large, airy and completely spotless room was a pleasant surprise.

'I've forgotten pretty much everything I learnt,' Anil confessed. 'I tried brushing up a little last night, but it was pretty much a losing battle. By the way, what's a phool jhaadu?'

'A broom,' Anjali said. 'The kind made out of dried rushes that you use to sweep dust off the floor.'

'Ah, now I get it,' he said, looking relieved. 'My maid's been asking me for one and I wasn't sure whether she meant a bouquet or a magic wand.' Anjali couldn't help it—she burst out laughing as Anil took out his Hindi notebooks and sat down on one of the chairs in the balcony.

'Let's go over whatever we've done till date,' she

suggested. 'And perhaps you need to do some extra work over the next week or two.'

The doorbell rang just as Anil opened his notebook, and he groaned as he got up to answer it. 'If it's a courier guy, I'll need your help,' he said. 'I can never tell if they want to see some identification or if they're asking for money.'

'I'm not too good with those either,' Anjali said, remembering a tussle with a recent courier delivery boy who'd refused to hand over a parcel addressed to Sushil until she proved that she was his lawfully-wedded wife. 'And if he starts talking in Marathi, I'm probably even worse than you are.'

It wasn't a courier guy though—it was Anil's relationship manager from his bank. Slim and very spiffily dressed in skin-tight beige trousers and a pale-green Mango jacket, she was quite clearly besotted with Anil. She looked distinctly put out when she saw Anjali.

'I didn't realise you were married,' she said to Anil, glancing at the forms she carried in her hand. 'I remember asking you when you opened an account with us.'

'I'm umm...engaged,' Anil said, throwing Anjali a beseeching look before she could contradict him. 'Anjali, this is Shefali from my bank—she's very kindly helping me out with my investments.'

She was probably being paid a hefty salary by the bank for her kind help, but Shefali didn't look pleased at all to hear of the 'engagement'. However, within a few seconds, her professional side asserted itself and she sat down with them to take them through a series of incredibly boring potential investments.

'Poor girl,' Anjali said once Shefali was gone. 'Poor girl my foot,' Anil retorted. 'She's like a bloody barracuda. I think the sole reason she works in a bank is so that she can get to meet rich men. Phew, the room's still stinking of her scent.'

'I need to leave,' Anjali said regretfully. 'It's time to go pick up Gayatri from her class.'

'Do I see you next Thursday?' Anil asked, and she nodded. 'Yes,' she said. 'And you need to rejoin the regular Saturday classes as well. I'll be doing a few conversation exercises that need a larger group.'

'I'll be there,' he said. 'Sorry about today.'

Anjali was humming to herself as she got into the car. Anil's unexpressed admiration made her feel a lot better about herself. Over the years, she had gotten used to having at least one silent or not-so-silent admirer hanging in the background. Deven Khatri had been the last in a series of many before she went back to happy domesticity with Sushil. There was a buzz around being at the receiving end of a crush—it also had the advantage of not needing any form of acknowledgement or reciprocation.

◆

'Is it okay if I pay your fees next month?' Zina asked. Anjali sighed. This was exactly what Sushil had warned her of. 'I don't think that works for me, Zina,' she said. Zina bit her lip. The TV show was about to take off and she had spent a lot of money on clothes and shoes. 'I can get you amazing discounts at the salon,' she ventured, and Anjali just about stopped herself from laughing. Rehaan's salon was mystifyingly called Twist, and it catered to the very rich and the very famous—even with a seventy-five per cent discount, she'd end up spending more there than she did at her neighbourhood beauty parlour. 'Maybe you could just restart classes after a bit,' she suggested. 'It's not like you don't know the language, you just need to brush up on your grammar and accent.'

'Rehaan's promised me a speaking role in the show,' Zina said fretfully. 'I can do a part of it in English, but the producer says I'll need to speak in Hindi as well. My accent isn't good enough yet.'

'Maybe you could do that bit in Tamil or Kannadiga,' Anjali suggested heartlessly, and Zina scowled. 'Look, what if I pay you half the fees now, and get you a free haircut from Rehaan plus a pedicure at the salon? Does that work? Rehaan's amazing, he'll give you a totally different look.'

'I don't want a totally different look,' Anjali said, running her fingers through her shoulder-length hair. 'But I guess I could do with a trim. Okay, Zina, sounds like a deal.'

Rehaan groaned when he heard. 'Zina, of all the stupid deals to make! My day's completely booked, and I have a meeting with the producer in the evening. Why can't you do her hair?'

'Because I told her you'd do it,' Zina retorted. 'Come on Rehaan! I've been working my butt off for your show, and you're not even paying me extra for it.'

'You'll get paid when they start shooting,' he said, but they both knew she had a point. Rehaan flicked through his diary on his phone and said, 'I can slot her in at 6.00,' he said. 'Make sure she's on time.'

'Are you comfortable with a male pedicurist?' In Anjali's view, a male beautician was only a couple of steps removed from a male gynaecologist, but she didn't fuss. Her feet looked like she had spent the last week working on the fields anyway—maybe a woman wouldn't be able to deal with them without fainting. 'Sure,' she said, and Zina flitted away and came back followed by a brawny young man who looked as if he'd be more at home on a football field than a salon.

'Dilip will do your pedicure and by the time he's done, Rehaan will be free,' Zina said. 'I have to do Mrs Kapadia's roots, so I'll be back only after a while.' Anjali had an immediate mental image of Mrs Kapadia being planted in a pot like a tulsi plant while Zina watered her feet, and grinned. 'Take your time,' she said. 'I'll be fine.'

Dilip gave her a shy smile as he began to fill the pedicure basin with warm water. 'Zina goes to you for Hindi classes, doesn't she?' he asked. 'I bet she's a troublesome student.' Anjali laughed. 'No, she's actually very sincere,' she said. It was true. With the prospect of the TV series ahead of her, Zina worked harder than all the rest of Anjali's students put together. If she had to pick her worst student, it would have to be Daffy, who had a fine disdain for the gender distinctions that the language posed. 'How can daadhi be female?' she argued. 'Only men have beards, right?' As a result, her Hindi was now fluent, but also a source of constant amusement for her colleagues.

'Have you worked here long, Dilip?' Anjali asked, and he nodded. 'Zina and I joined together,' he said, and then added, 'Of course she's a lot more talented than I am. She's almost as good as Rehaan Sir now.' Which was presumably why she got to work on people's hair while Dilip was stuck with their feet.

'Will you be on the TV show as well?' Anjali asked curiously. Dilip shrugged. 'In the background maybe, for a couple of shots. Otherwise it's going to be all Rehaan and Zina.'

'I hope the director thinks her Hindi's good enough,' Anjali said. 'She's worked really hard.'

'Yeah, she even makes Ishaan help her practice,' Dilip said. 'Poor kid, I don't think he knew what he was getting into. It's tough being Zina's boyfriend.'

'He seems sweet,' Anjali said. 'Only isn't he a little...'

'Young for her?' Dilip grinned as he carefully put one of Anjali's feet back in the water and picked up the other. 'We tease her about it all the time, but honestly, he's the only man I've seen who's able to manage her.

Otherwise she changes fiancés as often as other women change shoes.'

A tall, saturnine man in the last chair made a sudden movement, and the girl who was cutting his hair looked down in concern. 'I'm sorry, Sir, did I hurt you with the scissors?' she asked, and he shook his head, his hands gripping the armrests convulsively. The girl gave him a nervous look. There was something odd about this particular customer, and she was relieved when his haircut was done, and he got up to go.

'Name please?' she asked as she prepared to make his bill.

'Shiven Dhaliwal,' he said and handed her two five-hundred rupee notes. 'Here you go, I'm in a bit of a hurry. Can't wait for the bill.'

'Sir!' she called out after him, but the salon doors had already shut behind his massive frame. She grimaced. 'The haircut was only six hundred,' she said. 'What do I do with the rest?'

'Keep it,' Dilip said. 'It'll make up for the twenty rupees tip Mrs Kapadia gave you.' Anjali made a mental note to tip Dilip at least a hundred. She wasn't sure about Rehaan—he owned the salon, so obviously she couldn't tip him, but as she wasn't paying him, she should definitely make some kind of gesture. Perhaps she could bake him some brownies or something and send them through Zina later—she could hardly offer him Hindi lessons.

Rehaan was halfway through styling Anjali's hair when

Zina emerged from the back room. 'Rehaan, I'm done, can I leave?' she asked and then, as she caught sight of Anjali's hair, said, 'Wow, that looks good.' Anjali stared at her in the mirror. 'What does?' she demanded. 'I've got pins stuck all through my hair, I've no idea what's happening.'

'Wait till he's done,' Zina advised. 'You'll look like a supermodel, no one will guess you're a behenji from Bhopal. So can I go, Rehaan?'

Rehaan nodded, and she danced out of the salon with a flurry of bags and parcels. Rehaan caught Anjali's eye in the mirror and they burst out laughing simultaneously. 'Tactful, isn't she?' Rehaan said. 'Just to put the record straight though, you don't look like a behenji at all. And there's nothing wrong with Bhopal anyway—my wife grew up there and we love the city.'

'I'm from Indore, actually,' Anjali said, feeling apologetic.

'Well anyway, I'm sure it's quite as nice. Here you go. Like it?'

Anjali surveyed herself in the mirror. Rehaan had wisely not gone for anything too drastic—her hair was still the same length, but the wild curls had been deftly shaped and styled, and he had smoothed serum into them so that they fell into softly waving ringlets. She looked younger and more sophisticated at the same time, and Zina was right—Rehaan's scissors had erased the last traces of behenji-ness from her appearance.

'It's perfect,' she said, meaning it. 'Thank you, Rehaan!'

'My pleasure,' he said. In spite of his grumbling before she turned up, he found that he liked Anjali—there was something very refreshing about her ready smile and ability to laugh at herself.

He reached across to a shelf next to a large gilt-framed mirror and picked two bottles of hair products. 'Here, these are for you,' he said, giving them to Anjali. 'And no, you can't pay for them. Just make sure Zina gets that Hindi accent right before her show.'

It was a pleasant evening and Zina had decided to walk to the Westside store on Hughes Road. She was meeting Ishaan later in the evening and she wanted to get him a T-shirt. A couple of days ago he told her that he'd rather be seen wearing a ballerina's tutu than anything purple. Immediately, Zina had decided to get him a purple T-shirt and make him wear it on their next date. It was the kind of nutty humour that he appreciated, and playing silly pranks made her feel more in control.

Every week, Zina told herself that she needed to break up with Ishaan. And every time she met him, she postponed the decision to the following week. He had become sort of an obsession—a harmless one, a bit like her addiction to black coffee and dark chocolate fudge, but very powerful all the same. She kept telling herself that there was nothing wrong in what they were doing, she could break it off the day she wanted to. Only so far, she hadn't wanted to, and neither had he.

She was crossing the road with a Westside plastic carrier clutched in one hand and her bag in the other when her phone rang. 'Hello,' she said, fishing it out and answering it without checking the display.

'It's Shiven,' a deep voice said, and Zina stopped in her tracks. 'Oh bloody hell,' she said to herself. Then she took a deep breath and put the phone back to her ear and listened to what he had to say.

Dear Nanaji,

I hope you're better now—has the cough gone? Mom got a new haircut. She looks nice, but a little different from what I'm used to.

We had our Math and Chemistry tests last week, and I topped the class in both. Or at least my marks were the highest, but there were others who got an A plus as well.

I didn't end up going to I magica after all. It wouldn't have been fun without Rhea, so I told Mom and Dad to postpone the trip. I wish I knew why Rhea is so upset with me. Perhaps I'll try to talk to her again like you suggested.

Love,
Gayatri

eight

'D'YOU HAVE Krish's mom's number?' Gayatri asked. Anjali looked up from the cake she was mixing. 'It's on my phone,' she said. 'Kavita Askandani.'

Gayatri called the number from her own phone but couldn't get through. 'Home number?' she asked peremptorily, and Anjali sighed. Five months ago, she would have refused to answer unless Gayatri said 'please'—now it didn't seem worth the inevitable tantrum. 'Check the calling list on my pin-board,' she said. Gayatri wandered off and came back frowning. 'No one's picking up,' she said fretfully. 'Krish borrowed my Science notes and said he'd get them back to me by evening. I need them now!'

'Why did you lend them to him in the first place?' Anjali asked.

'He was absent for a couple of days,' Gayatri said sullenly. 'Ate himself silly at a wedding and got sick. Can you try his mom once?'

Anjali got through to Kavita on the first attempt. Kavita was hugely apologetic. 'I'm terribly sorry,' she said. 'I'm not at home though—I'm in Juhu for a puja at a friend's place, and my car and driver are with me. Is there any way you could get the notes picked up? Krish didn't say a word about needing to return them today, or I'd have dropped them back on my way to the suburbs.'

'I'll send my driver,' Anjali said. 'Is Krish at home? No one was picking up the phone.'

'Yes, he is. The landline's been acting up for the last few days. I'm really sorry about this, Anjali. I'll give Krish an earful when I get home.'

'Can I go with Tiwari?' Gayatri demanded. Anjali shook her head. After the hangover episode, Tiwari had been as good as gold, but sending a young girl alone with a driver wasn't safe.

'What if he gets the wrong notebook? And I'm getting bored here anyway. I can do my homework with Krish if he's home.'

Anjali hesitated. 'Take Lalita with you,' she said finally. Lalita was the daughter of Anjali's maid in Indore, and she had moved to Mumbai with them to help Anjali with work around the house.

Gayatri made a face but agreed. Krish's house was only a few kilometres away. If they'd still been in Indore, Gayatri could have cycled the distance, but Mumbai traffic made it impossible.

It took almost forty-five minutes to get to Krish's house, and Gayatri stared broodingly out of the window for most of the way. Things at school were getting worse—Rhea had started avoiding her, and even some of the boys had started snickering when she put up her hand when a teacher asked a question. Wellington students were known for their relaxed, laid-back approach to their studies—the school encouraged children to research and learn on their own rather than mug up for exams. Gayatri's old school had been a traditional one, and she was used to working hard and topping her class. Her grades continued to be excellent but she knew she was handling things all wrong, and she didn't know how to fix it.

'*Lalita didi, aap gaadi mein ruko,*' Gayatri told the maid once they reached the lobby of the apartment.

Krish gave her a toothy grin when he came to answer the door. 'What an enthu kid you are,' he remarked.

Gayatri shook her head. 'No, I won't come in. Thanks for the notes. Hope you managed to copy them out.'

She was halfway to the lift when she turned back and asked with an air of assumed casualness, 'Which floor does Alisha Mehta live on?'

Krish frowned. 'Fourth floor. Hang on, Gayatri, you can't...' But Gayatri was already running up the stairs. Her heart was thumping like a metronome on steroids as she reached the fourth floor. It was a wild shot, but she had to give it a try. Alisha's disapproval was what had got her into a mess in the first place—perhaps if she went and apologised, Alisha would understand that she had not meant to be rude or cruel. And if Alisha's mother was around, perhaps she'd intervene and insist that Alisha be friends with her, and then perhaps, the other girls would stop tormenting her.

She rang the bell and waited for a bit. There seemed to be no movement inside the flat, though there was light seeping out from under the door. After around a minute, she rang the bell again and this time, she could hear footsteps coming towards the door.

'Hi,' a vaguely familiar male voice said, and Gayatri looked up to see Alisha's older brother smiling at her. 'Are you here to see Alisha?' Gayatri nodded and blushed. She had hoped Alisha would come to the door—it would be difficult explaining to anyone else exactly why she was here. Also, she had a bit of a crush on Ishaan ever since she met him at Palladium with Zina. It would be extremely embarrassing if his sister told him the reason behind her visit.

'She isn't home right now, but she'll be back in a few minutes,' Ishaan said. 'Why don't you come in and wait? She's just gone downstairs to walk Tughlaq.'

Tughlaq was Alisha's Labrador, and a big favourite in school. Before the whole fracas began, Alisha had brought him to the inter-house Sports Meet and Gayatri had played with him for hours.

'How's Tugs?' she asked as she followed Ishaan into the flat, not bothering to ask him if anyone else was at home—the umpteen lectures that Anjali had given her on never being alone with a strange man had completely slipped her mind. Even if she did remember them, she'd have thought them not relevant to the present situation.

'Tugs is brilliant as always,' Ishaan said, turning to smile at her, and Gayatri thought, yet again, about how nice he looked. 'Growing a bit old.'

The living room of the Mehtas' flat was large and beautifully done up in shades of blue and ivory—Gayatri looked around with a little gasp of wonder. 'It's such a pretty room,' she said involuntarily, and Ishaan laughed.

'I can't take any credit for it unfortunately. Now what will you have—juice, cold drink, ginger beer?'

'Ginger beer,' Gayatri said promptly, and Ishaan fetched a can from the kitchen. His fingers touched hers briefly as he handed it to her and Gayatri found herself blushing again. Struggling to look composed and unaffected, she reminded herself sternly that Ishaan was *years* older than her, and was Zina's boyfriend. For Gayatri, Zina was the epitome of sophistication—sometimes, after a particularly bad fight with Anjali, she daydreamed about growing up and moving out of her parents' home to live with a flatmate like Zina. On Saturdays, she hung around to see what Zina was wearing to the Hindi class. A couple of times, she had even gone out in to the passageway and tried on Zina's shoes that were lying there, noticing with a little thrill of excitement that Zina's foot size was exactly the same as hers.

'Haven't I seen you before?' Ishaan was asking. 'You're Anjali's daughter, aren't you?'

Gayatri was about to say yes when the doorbell rang. 'That must be Alisha,' Ishaan said, getting up to answer the door. But it wasn't. Hearing raised voices a few minutes later, Gayatri tiptoed into the hall. There was a huge man at the door and he looked really angry.

Ishaan was leaning against the door jamb, a mocking smile on his lips. 'I don't get it, Mr Dhaliwal,' he said, stretching out the name so that it sounded like an insult. 'What exactly is bothering you about my relationship with Zina?'

'It's not something I would like to discuss at the door like this,' the man said. 'Zina is a close friend, and I can't talk about her personal matters where anyone can overhear us.'

'You're welcome to come in.' Ishaan shifted from the door and ushered Shiven into the hall. Gayatri slipped back into the living room before either of the men noticed her.

'Are you planning to marry her?'

The question was so abrupt and serious that Ishaan was taken off-guard for a moment. Recovering quickly, he said, 'I don't see how that concerns you.'

'It concerns me all right,' Shiven said grimly.

Ishaan shrugged. 'If you say so. I don't think I want to discuss it though. Perhaps you should speak to Zina about it since you know her so well?'

'I'm asking you,' Shiven said, his voice rising as he gripped the younger man's shoulder with his large and sinewy hands. 'And I'm not going away until you tell me.' Ishaan twisted away from him with a sudden movement. 'I'd recommend you keep your hands off me,' he said, his voice as cold as ice.

'Then I'd recommend you stay away from Zina,' Shiven roared. 'I know what you rich kids are like—you'll play the fool with her for a while, and then you'll head off to the US leaving her behind. How dare you touch her, you...you little pup, you're not good enough to breathe the same air as her, I can't believe you had the audacity to actually...' He broke off, his broad chest heaving with mingled anger and frustration.

Ishaan's forehead had furrowed as Shiven started off—at being called a 'little pup', however, his expression cleared and he gave a little snort of laughter. 'I'm sorry,' he said as Shiven glared at him. 'But really... It's not like Zina's some innocent village maiden, is she? She's been around quite a bit and she isn't any more serious about me than I am about her. Come on, Mr Dhaliwal, try and see it from my point of view. I'm twenty-one. Is it likely I'd tie myself up getting married to a girl seven years older than me?'

Shiven stared down at the boy's handsome laughing face in dumb fury, realising that every word of what he said was true. He hadn't seduced Zina, and Zina was perfectly aware of the fact that the chances of their getting married were dim. Still, she chose him over Shiven and the stable, happy marriage he was offering her. The boy was still saying something, but Shiven couldn't hear him any longer, as a wave of irrational fury swept over him.

'Mr Dhaliwal?' Ishaan said, and Shiven drew back a massive fist and punched him in the stomach. Shiven was almost a foot taller and thirty-five kilos heavier, plus he had the advantage of surprise—Ishaan didn't stand a chance.

Gayatri heard the sound of the blow and ran to the door of the living room. She was just in time to see Ishaan stagger back against the wall, completely winded, while Shiven followed up the first blow with a series of lethal punches till Ishaan slumped to the floor, doubled up in agony. It was the first time Gayatri had seen violence up close, and she was too shocked even to scream. She clung to the door, whimpering softly. Something alerted Shiven to the fact that there was someone else in the house. He stopped and turned to look into the eyes of the terrified girl. They stared at each other for almost a minute and the red haze slowly lifted from Shiven's brain leaving a dull heaviness behind. He swung around and let himself out of the flat, not even turning to look at the huddled body on the floor.

The door slammed behind Shiven, and Gayatri slowly moved away from the door frame she'd been clinging to and began to edge towards the main door. Ishaan looked up, his eyes clouded over with pain, and he said, 'Please...' and stretched a hand towards her.

Later, she couldn't explain what happened to her in that instant—perhaps it was the shock, or the way Ishaan looked, his body twisted in pain and blood oozing from a cut on his head, but she edged past him and ran out of the main door, down the staircase and into the waiting car.

'*Ghar chalo,*' she said, and neither Lalita nor Tiwari realised that anything was wrong. Tiwari started the car, and Gayatri took her phone out of her pocket with trembling hands and dialled Krish's home number.

'Something happened at Alisha's house,' she said when he picked up. 'A man came in and attacked her brother. Can you call someone?'

She put the phone down and stared blindly out of the window. The memory of Ishaan's hand almost touching her foot as she ran out of the flat kept playing over and over in her mind in an endless loop. And the other man's face—for a second when he turned, she had thought he was about to attack her.

The traffic on Peddar Road was even worse on the way back, and twenty minutes later, they'd hardly moved. Gayatri pulled out her phone and dialled Krish's number again. 'Is he okay?' she asked as soon as Krish picked up the phone.

'Alisha and Tugs had just found him when I went up,' Krish said. 'They've called an ambulance and they'll take him to Breach Candy or to Jaslok, whichever they can get to faster. Do you know what happened? He's unconscious, he can't tell them anything.'

'I saw a man running out of the building, that's all,' Gayatri said and put the phone down.

When Gayatri finally got home, Anjali had stepped out to a neighbour's place to return a CD she had borrowed, and Sushil was on a call. Lalita heated up dinner quickly, and Gayatri was able to eat and go to bed without her parents figuring out that anything was wrong.

It was eleven at night when Kavita Askandani got back from the puja and Krish told her what had happened. He tried calling her earlier, but their landline had finally given up the ghost, and his grandmother was too nervous to let him go out and call from a neighbour's phone.

'But did she see the man?' Kavita asked. 'She must have, right, otherwise she wouldn't have called you and asked you to check.' Krish shrugged. 'No clue,' he said. 'She sounded pretty freaked out though when she called.'

Kavita hesitated a little. It was a bit too late to call Anjali, and anyway, Gayatri would have told her what had happened. 'How badly is Ishaan hurt?' she asked Krish.

'Nimisha Aunty said his appendix is ruptured,' Krish said, and Kavita stared at him in dismay. 'But that's serious!' she said. 'Will you go to bed now, sweetheart? I just want to run upstairs and ask them if they need any help.'

The door to the Mehtas' flat was open—the police were just leaving. 'We'll take a statement as soon as he's well enough to talk,' one of the policemen was saying to Ishaan's uncle. 'There's not much we can do till then.'

'Thank you,' Dr Shah said politely. 'I'll call as soon as we have some news from the hospital.' He was Dr Suhasini's older brother, and after Ishaan's father died, he devoted himself to helping the family pull themselves together.

Kavita went up to Dr Shah as he was about to shut the door. 'Hi, Suhasini introduced us a few months ago,' she said. 'I live on the first floor—I just heard. Is there anything at all I can do? Does Alisha need anything?'

'Maybe you could try talking to her,' Dr Shah said. 'She's still in shock, but she's insisting that she wants to be in the hospital with Ishaan.'

Alisha was sitting in the living room, tears rolling silently down her cheeks. The big Labrador was sitting dolefully at her feet and she was stroking his furry back mechanically.

'Beta, why don't you go to bed?' Kavita said, coming and sitting down next to her. 'We'll call you as soon as we get some news.'

Alisha shook her head. 'I want to go to Ishaan,' she said.

'But who'll look after Tugs then? He's as upset as you are, poor fellow, and your uncle's not very comfortable with dogs, is he?'

'I'll take him with me,' Alisha said desperately. 'Aunty, please, he'll wait in the car. He's very, very good. I need to be with Ishaan—this is all my fault!'

Understandably surprised, Kavita stared at Alisha.

'But...how could it be your fault, sweetheart? You weren't even here, were you?'

'I wasn't. I took Tugs down for a walk, and he wanted to come home, but I got talking to one of my friends in the next building.' She took a deep, sobbing breath. 'If I'd come back in time, Tugs would have killed the guy before he touched Ishaan, and Ishaan wouldn't have been in hospital... So you see, it *is* all my fault. Mom keeps telling me to make sure I get home on time and not stand around gossiping, and I never listen to her, and now look at what's happened...' She dissolved into tears and Kavita pulled her close, patting her shoulder gently.

'Shh,' she said. 'This won't help Ishaan, sweetie. Come on now, let's tidy this room up and after that let's pack an overnight bag for your mom. She'll probably need to stay with Ishaan in the hospital for a few days. And I'll ask Krish's dad to look after Tugs in the morning and I'll take you to the hospital. Come on now, get up.'

The thought of doing something practical got Alisha onto her feet. The rugs on the floor were askew as they'd been indiscriminately trodden on by the policemen and there was a puddle on the floor where Gayatri's half-empty can of ginger beer had been knocked over. Alisha used a mop to clean up the mess, and then frowned at the ginger beer. 'I wonder why this is here,' she remarked. 'Ishaan hates ginger beer. Should we go and put mom's things together, Kavita Aunty? This room's done for now.'

'There's one of your notebooks lying on the sofa,'

Kavita pointed out. 'Put that into your school bag and then we can start on your mom's packing.'

'This isn't mine,' Alisha said, frowning at the green notebook with the Wellington crest on the front cover. 'Did Krish leave it here?' She picked up the notebook and opened it, and stiffened immediately. 'Gayatri Dubey,' she said slowly. 'Now what's this doing here?'

'She came to pick up a notebook from Krish,' Kavita said, frowning. 'And she called Krish to say that she saw a man running away from your flat. Maybe Krish brought it here when he came upstairs? Only as far as I know, this is the notebook she came here to take.'

'Aunty, can I talk to Krish?' Alisha asked. Kavita started to say that he'd be asleep, but one look at Alisha's tense face was enough to make her change her mind.

'Gayatri did ask which floor you lived on,' Krish said, sleepily rubbing his eyes. 'But if you weren't home, she wouldn't have gone into your flat. Anyway, it's not like you guys were the best of friends.'

'I need to talk to Gayatri,' Alisha said, her face white and set. 'She was here, I know she was. That's why the ginger beer can was in the living room.'

'Alisha, even if she was here, she couldn't have seen what happened,' Kavita said. 'I'll call her mother in the morning, all right?'

'I want to speak to her now,' Alisha said. 'Krish, go and get me her number.'

'No, wait,' Kavita said. 'I'll call her mother now. But

I'll allow you to speak to Gayatri only if her mother is okay with it.'

Both Sushil and Anjali were fast asleep when Anjali's phone rang. Anjali sat up and frowned at the display. 'Why's she calling me?' she muttered, and Sushil grunted, 'You should keep your phone switched off at night.'

'Hi, Kavita?' Anjali said, slipping out of bed. 'No, I'd just fallen asleep. No, that's okay... What? No, I'm sure you're mistaken... Krish must have misunderstood what she said—my maid and driver were with her, one of them would have told me... No, Alisha cannot speak to her right now. I understand she's upset, but my daughter is asleep, and I don't plan to wake her... What d'you mean, it's a police matter?' Her voice rose in alarm, and Sushil sat up in bed. 'I'll wake her up and ask her... How's he doing now? Oh God, his poor mother. I hope he recovers... Let me know if there's anything we can do to help. And I'll speak to Gayatri right away and call you back.'

Sushil was out of bed now, standing next to her. Anjali turned troubled eyes up to him. 'Either Kavita's drunk, or I'm going mad,' she said helplessly. 'She's saying that a boy was attacked in their building, and Gayatri was there. But Gayatri didn't breathe a word about it.'

'We'll have to wake her up and ask her,' Sushil said. 'Relax, there's probably a simple explanation.' But when they snapped the light on in Gayatri's room and found her lying in bed wide-awake, they knew that the explanation wasn't going to be simple at all.

◆

Ishaan's condition was still critical—his appendix had ruptured under the second blow, and there was a risk of peritonitis. His mother had pulled every string she could to get him into a state-of-the-art operation theatre with the best possible surgeons operating on him, but it was still touch and go. 'At least there's no other major injury,' one of the doctors told Dr Suhasini. 'Though there's severe trauma in the area—whoever attacked him seems to have been a professional boxer. All the blows were concentrated in a small area and the force he used was immense.'

'I don't care if he was a professional sumo wrestler,' Dr Suhasini said tautly. 'The second I find out who he is, he'll be behind bars. Do you think my boy will be okay, Dhruv?'

But Dr Dhruv refused to commit himself. They'd done their best and now the rest was up to God. So Dr Suhasini went into her consulting room on the third floor of the hospital and got down on her knees and prayed continuously, with breaks only to go upstairs to the ICU and check if anything had changed.

Zina found out only the next morning when Sushil finally made the connection between her and Ishaan and called her. 'Oh God,' she said, and again, 'Oh God.'

'Zina, is Shiven's surname Dhaliwal? Because that's the name Gayatri heard.'

'It is,' Zina said. 'Sushil, I've been so criminally stupid…' 'There's nothing you can do about that now,' Sushil said. 'We'll figure out the Shiven angle later. D'you want me to come and pick you up? Does Ishaan's family know about you?'

They didn't, or at least Dr Suhasini didn't. Alisha probably did, but she was sedated now and at home, and the hospital staff refused to allow Zina up to the ICU waiting room.

'Come and wait at our place,' Sushil said finally when Zina called him. 'Anjali's planning to go to the hospital in a while to check on Ishaan. There's no point in you going all the way back to Bandra.'

Zina nodded before she realised Sushil couldn't see her. 'I'll hang around here for a bit in case I can get some news,' she said. 'I'll be at your place by around eleven if that's okay?'

'Yes, of course Zina can come here,' Anjali said, sounding distracted. Gayatri's story had shaken her up badly, and she was pacing up and down the living room not knowing what to do. She had met Ishaan only once, but she really liked him—it was terrible to think of all that vitality and charm quenched. Kavita had told her that they weren't yet sure if he'd make it, and she hadn't bothered to hide her disapproval of Gayatri's behaviour.

'I can't believe you didn't tell me,' Anjali said for about the twentieth time in the day, and Gayatri finally snapped.

'I'd have told you if you were in the least bit interested in what happens to me,' she said. 'But as you were busy gossiping with the neighbours, I thought I'd let it go.'

Anjali reared back as if she had been slapped. She had always been a hands-on mum, and now that she wasn't working full-time any more, she tried to be as involved in Gayatri's life as possible. Being accused of disinterest was as hurtful as it could possibly get.

'Let it go,' Sushil said softly as Anjali opened her mouth to retaliate. Gayatri stared defiantly at both of them for a bit, then turned and ran to her room.

'I've made such a hash of this move,' Anjali muttered, sinking into the nearest sofa. 'I knew she was having trouble adjusting, but I purposely stayed out of it because I thought she needed to handle it on her own. And the last few weeks she's been very quiet and she's cut me off every time I try speaking to her...' 'It's a tough age,' Sushil said. He had been acutely conscious of the years he lived away from his daughter, and he had not interfered with Anjali's parenting style even when he thought she was making mistakes. 'Maybe we should try talking to her more, being more like friends than parents?'

'I'm rubbish at that kind of stuff,' Anjali said. 'Can you try, Sushil? She's a lot freer with you than she is with me.'

The telephone bell rang, and Sushil went to pick it up.

'Is Gayatri at home?'

'Yes,' Sushil said. 'Who's this?'

'I'm a classmate of hers,' Alisha said, banking on the fact that over the telephone, Gayatri's father wouldn't be able to tell the difference between a teenager and a twelve-year-old. Quite likely he wouldn't be able to tell the difference face to face either—fathers were notoriously unobservant.

Sushil hesitated a little and then took the cordless to Gayatri's room. Hopefully, talking to a friend would cheer her up.

'Hello,' Gayatri said listlessly, expecting it to be Nivi or Shweta, the two nice but completely boring girls she was reduced to hanging around with nowadays.

'Gayatri?' The voice was of an older girl, vaguely familiar, but she wasn't able to place it immediately. 'Yes?' she said, wondering if it was Rhea's sister calling to say that Rhea wanted to make up for their quarrel.

'Just to let you know that I think you're an absolute bitch,' the voice said, dripping with venom. 'I'd actually begun to feel a little sorry for you because your best friend ditched you, but now I'm going to make sure the entire school stops talking to you.'

'Alisha...' Gayatri said faintly, but there was no stopping her.

'You were *there*...and you left my brother lying on the floor when you could have gone and called for help—what kind of a person are you?' In Alisha's mind, the time gap between Gayatri running out of the flat and Ishaan's being found had expanded to an absolutely unforgiveable extent.

'He might die because you didn't call someone in time! People like you don't deserve to live in a civilised society.' It was something Alisha had heard her mom say about white-collar criminals and the phrase had stuck in her mind. Tears were running down her cheeks again, and she brushed them away angrily.

'Don't think I'm going to forget this, because I'm not,' she said. 'Just wait till you're back in school.' She banged the receiver down, and Gayatri hung up, shaking in reaction. Till now, she had not realised exactly how irresponsible she had been in her panic—the time factor of getting medical help hadn't occurred to her. To be fair, when it had been happening, she hadn't realised how badly Ishaan was hurt—she thought he was just winded—and was so scared of the man coming back that she ran for her life. No one seemed to understand that though, not even her mother.

'I think I'll go to the hospital,' Anjali said, getting to her feet. 'Tell Zina to wait for me—it'll be visiting hours in a short while, maybe they'll let us in.'

Zina was standing in the hospital lobby, looking so lost that for the first time since they'd met, Anjali actually felt sorry for her.

'Aren't they letting you in?' she asked, and Zina shook her head. 'I don't even know where he is,' she said, her voice breaking. 'Could you ask that friend of yours?'

Thankfully, Kavita was disposed to be helpful. 'He's still in the ICU,' she said. 'Sushasini's in the hospital—she has a consulting room on the second floor. You'll find her there.'

Anjali thanked her and ran off. 'I think we should try and find his mother,' she told Zina. 'Maybe she'll be okay with meeting you, and you'll know exactly what's happening with Ishaan.'

Or maybe she'd want to throttle her once she found out that she was responsible for her son being in the ICU, Zina thought, but she didn't say it out loud. Somehow, she thought Anjali would be a lot less understanding than Sushil, and Zina needed her help.

'Hi Anjali, everything okay? Are you here to see a patient?' Anjali had been biting her lip trying to think of the best way to get to meet Dr Suhasini, and she gave a gasp of relief as she saw Anil.

'To inquire about one,' she said. 'Ishaan Mehta, he was in the ICU.'

'Ah, Dr Suhasini's son,' Anil's expression turned sombre. 'I heard they got him here just in time—another few minutes and he'd have been gone. As it is he's in a pretty critical condition.'

Anjali's stomach clenched in reaction. So Kavita hadn't been over-reacting the previous night. Gayatri's running away was completely inexcusable.

'Is there any way of getting to meet her?' Anjali gestured towards Zina. 'Zina's a close friend of Ishaan's, and she's very worried about him.'

Anil looked dubious. 'I'm not sure if they're allowing people in to meet her,' he said. 'But let me see what I can do. I have a consulting room on the same floor as hers.'

'I'm so sorry to intrude, Dr Suhasini,' Anjali said. Anil had managed to get them some time with her, though he warned them that they shouldn't stay for long. Suhasini looked like she had aged a decade in the previous night—she was rigidly in control of herself, but her hands trembled slightly as she ushered them in.

'Zina's a good friend of Ishaan's and she was very worried about him,' Anjali added. Zina looked at Ishaan's mother nervously. People reacted oddly under stress—was Ishaan's mother about to start screaming at her? Even if she didn't know about Shiven, the fact that a twenty-seven-year-old woman was playing around with her twenty-year-old son might be enough to set her off. Anjali's 'friend' story wasn't fooling anyone.

To Zina's surprise, Dr Suhasini's expression softened, and she said, 'Yes, Alisha did say that we should inform you. But Ishaan password-locks his phone and she wasn't able to get your number.' She sighed. 'What a way to find out that my son's been dating someone. But that's kids for you nowadays—they tell you nothing.' She smiled at Zina. 'Come and sit down, my girl. I don't have much news for you unfortunately. He's still in the ICU—they operated on him last night and now they're waiting for him to wake up.'

Zina sat down in the chair indicated, and then to her own complete horror, she burst into tears. Anjali got up to go to her, but Dr Suhasini motioned to her to sit down and let Zina get on with it. She pushed a box of tissues across to Zina and waited till the worst of it was over. 'I'm so sorry,' Zina said, wiping her eyes after one last shuddering sob. 'You're his mother, I can only imagine how you must be feeling...'

'I'm feeling very, very angry,' Dr Suhasini said surprisingly. 'With the man who did this to my son. And I'm scared because I'm not sure if Ishaan will pull through. But that doesn't mean I don't understand what you're going through.'

If she had been even slightly rude or condescending, Zina wouldn't have said a thing, but now she couldn't bear to stay silent.

'I know who did it,' she said abruptly, and as Anjali turned to stare at her, the whole story came tumbling out.

♦

Dr Suhasini was a saint, Anjali thought confusedly, once Zina ground to a halt. In her place, anyone else would be storming around and cursing, but she just looked a little thoughtful as she pushed the box of tissues back towards Zina.

'I can see why you're blaming yourself, but it's quite unnecessary,' she said crisply. 'Both Dhaliwal and Ishaan are grown men—or at least, Ishaan is almost grown up.'

It was the only reference she had made so far to her son's extreme youth, and Zina bit her lip. 'And relationships nowadays are a lot more complicated than they used to be. You're no more responsible for what happened than I am.'

The phone rang on her desk and Dr Suhasini turned to pick it up. 'Right…' they heard her say. 'Right…thank you, doctor…thank you so much.'

When she put the phone down, her eyes were shining with relief.

'He's out of danger,' she said. 'They'll move him out of the ICU in the afternoon and he should be ready to go home next week.'

At this, Zina promptly burst into tears again, and this time, Dr Suhasini came around the table and hugged her.

'See, you brought him good luck,' she said, making Anjali want to point out to Dr Suhasini that if Zina hadn't meddled with her son, he wouldn't have been in hospital in the first place. 'We should leave now,' she said instead. 'You'll need to go and be with Ishaan, won't you?'

'Come over tomorrow morning and see him,' Dr Suhasini said to Zina as they got up. 'And if you leave your number with me, I'll call you in the evening and tell you how he is.'

'I don't get this,' Sushil said slowly to Zina once they got home. 'I thought you broke up with Shiven—you walked out of the wedding, didn't you? Are you saying you were dating him secretly all along?'

'He kept calling me and making extravagant gestures like putting up those hoardings opposite your flat.'

'Hoardings opposite your flat?' Anjali asked, her eyes as big as saucers. Sushil waved a hand at her. 'I'll tell you all about it later,' he said. 'Young Zina collects some really colourful admirers.'

'Well, anyway, I didn't take it very seriously,' Zina said. 'I've always thought that people who make grand gestures aren't really as terribly in love as they pretend to be. That hoarding stuff stopped being funny after a bit, so I told him that he needed to back off because I was absolutely sure I didn't want to have anything to do with him. And he was very understanding, he said he knew he had gone over the top, and he was sorry, couldn't we just be friends again...'

Sushil rolled his eyes and she looked defensive. 'Well how was I to know that he was bluffing?'

'Maybe the fact that he was all set to marry you a month before that should have given you a clue,' Sushil murmured, but Anjali elbowed him. 'Let her finish,' she said. 'I want to understand this.'

'I never thought I'd see you take her side over mine,' Sushil said sorrowfully, but he subsided when both women glared at him.

'Then you told me that I needed to move out and I started looking for a place. And Shiven heard about it, and he came and fed me all this bullshit about wanting me to be comfortable and happy, and how the rent was peanuts for him... I thought he was crazy, saying he'd pay my rent when he knew I didn't care two hoots about him. But the offer was too good to pass and it wasn't like he was expecting me to sleep with him or anything in return.'

'Hmmm,' Sushil said. He understood how Zina's brain functioned better than most people, and while he didn't condone what she did, he wasn't about to start criticising either. 'So as soon as you were all set up in this flat that he was paying for, you went and found yourself a hot young lover.'

Zina groaned. 'It wasn't quite like that,' she said. 'This whole thing with Ishaan wasn't meant to happen. It was all spur-of-the-moment stuff and I never thought it would last.'

'It hasn't,' Sushil pointed out. 'The poor boy's lying in hospital half-dead while your ex tramps around town looking for more people to beat up.'

'Stop it, Sushil,' Anjali said sharply. 'Zina, how did Shiven find out about Ishaan?'

'Overheard some people talking,' Zina said glumly. 'And when he called me, I panicked a bit and said that we'd slept together a few times, but it was over now.' She took a deep breath. 'I think he might have got the impression that Ishaan dumped me.'

'And so he went charging off to sort the guy out???' Sushil gave a low whistle. 'Ahh, that explains a lot. Why didn't Ishaan just explain though? I don't know how much Gayatri overheard or understood, but from what she said, it sounded like he was going out of his way to annoy Shiven.'

'It's the kind of thing he'd find funny,' Zina explained. 'He's a bit weird like that.'

'I'll never understand this generation,' Sushil said. 'Though I must say the boy has balls, needling a guy that size. I've never seen a human being who looks more like King Kong. What're you going to do about the flat, Z?'

'I'm moving out today,' Zina said. Sushil raised his eyebrows. 'And going where?'

'Could I stay with you guys for a couple of days?' she asked hopefully. 'Just till I find something?'

But Sushil was already shaking his head. 'Sorry, Zina,' he said. 'Not when your ex-fiancé is likely to turn up any moment and pound one of us to pulp. I can see I've had a lucky escape when you stayed with me in Bandra.'

'He knew there wasn't anything happening between us,' Zina said. 'And he knows that Anjali and Gayatri are back, so he won't come.'

'How reassuring,' Sushil remarked. 'Thanks, but no thanks. I'll lend you money to stay at a hotel for a few days if you want.'

'Ignore him,' Anjali said. 'You can stay here until you figure something out. Right, Sushil?'

'No, she can't,' Sushil said. 'Seriously, Anjali, you don't know what Shiven will do next, and I'll be away at work.'

'Rubbish, nothing's going to happen,' Anjali said.

'Why is it always me?' Sushil asked Zina plaintively.

'Because you're the only rich guy with a big flat I know.'

'What about Rehaan?'

'I asked him. His wife's having a baby, and the due date's only a month away.'

'Trust you to go and work for the only non-gay celebrity hairdresser in town,' Sushil muttered. He thought for a bit. 'Look, you can stay here for a while, but if there's the slightest risk, out you go, okay?'

Zina's eyes lit up, and he frowned. 'Just for a week, and after that, you need to make arrangements of your own.'

Gayatri slid back into her room before her mother could come into the corridor and find her. She couldn't believe her parents were actually comforting Zina and giving her a place to stay when the whole mess had actually been Zina's fault—she said so herself.

The next morning, Zina changed into a sunflower yellow top and white capris and set off for the hospital, her heart thumping in trepidation. It was all very well being forgiven by Dr Suhasini, but it was more than likely that Ishaan wouldn't be quite as forgiving. She had never told him about Shiven, beyond telling him that she broke an earlier engagement off—nothing she said would have prepared him for someone landing up on his doorstep and attacking him.

Ishaan looked pale and tired, and there was a drip going into his arm, and all kinds of scary-looking paraphernalia around his hospital bed. Even his eyes, normally so alive and snapping with mischief were dull, and his movements as he reached for a glass of water were sluggish.

Zina hesitated on the threshold feeling suddenly very close to tears. 'Ishaan?' she said, and he looked around, his face lighting up so that he looked a lot more like his usual self.

'Hey Zina,' he said. 'Where's my purple T-shirt, girl?'

'I forgot to get it,' Zina said, crossing the room to his side and taking his hand. 'I'm so sorry, Ishaan. This is all my fault.'

'You're the third person who's come here and said that,' Ishaan remarked, lifting her hand and brushing it lightly with his lips. 'Unfortunately, not one of them has been Shiven Dhaliwal.'

'And you're still refusing to file an FIR,' a teenage girl sitting on the attendant's couch said. 'I don't understand you. A guy like that is dangerous—he should be locked up for the rest of his life!'

Zina hadn't really registered the presence of another human being in the room, but she turned and looked at the girl now, noticing her startling resemblance to Ishaan. They had the same swooping eyebrows and flashing eyes, and the girl's skin was as flawless though she was a lot darker than Ishaan.

'It's complicated, Ally,' Ishaan was saying. 'There were...mitigating circumstances. And think how stupid I would feel, the whole world knowing that I got beaten up and put into hospital.'

Alisha rolled her eyes. 'The guy was the size of a gorilla.'

'Yes, but I'm a karate black belt,' Ishaan pointed out. 'Ally, d'you want to go and grab something to eat in the cafeteria? Zina will sit with me till you're back.'

'Yeah okay,' Alisha said, standing up and stretching. She gave Zina a stern look. 'He's still recovering—don't be up to any mischief while I'm away, okay?'

'Okay,' Zina said, a bit stunned. Alisha was around ten years younger than her, and around ten times as confident. Clearly the new generation knew something that hers didn't.

'Come here,' Ishaan said, as soon as the door shut behind Alisha, and Zina went gratefully into his arms, burying her face in his neck. His hospital-issued clothes smelt of soap and disinfectant, but he obviously got someone to fetch him his own aftershave and cologne because his skin smelt the way it always did—citrus with an exciting hint of spice. He shifted slightly, and pressed his lips against Zina's cheek, and she turned and sought his mouth blindly with her own.

After a few seconds, Ishaan eased away from her, his hands coming up to frame her face as he looked into her eyes. 'Are you crying?' he asked in consternation. 'What's wrong, Zina? I swear I'm fine I'll be out of here in a day or two.'

'I know,' Zina said, wiping her eyes with her fingers. 'But you could have died, and...and...'

'And it would have been all your fault,' he said. 'I

know. But I didn't die, so it's fine, isn't it?' He reached out to the bedside table and grabbed a box of tissues. 'Here you go,' he said. 'And now, pull up a chair and come and sit next to me—you'll get rheumatism, leaning over and crying buckets like that.'

'Right, sorry,' Zina said as she realised that Ishaan's shoulder was wet with her tears. 'When are they letting you out?'

'Next week if I'm lucky.' He gave her a quick grin. 'Why, missing me already?'

'Just a little. Ishaan, why aren't you filing that FIR?'

His expression closed up immediately. 'It's not worth making a fuss about.'

'But it is! He can't get away with something like this!' Zina was almost jiggling with frustration. She hadn't spoken to Shiven because she didn't want to warn him, but she was dying to see him punished.

'Look, there's no way we can get him convicted without raking up a whole lot of mud,' he said. 'Better to let it be.'

Zina stared at him, comprehension slowly dawning on her. 'You mean, because I'd get dragged into it? Oh, but that makes no sense, Ishaan! And what if he does it again?'

He touched her hand lightly. 'He won't. My mother discussed it with my uncle, and he's speaking to a few people. I don't think there's any risk of it happening again.'

It sounded very Mafia-like, but he refused to talk about it any longer and he was beginning to look exhausted, so Zina contented herself with holding his hand and dropping light kisses on his cheek every few minutes. He had dosed off by the time Alisha came back to the room, and she gave them a disappointed look.

'Here I thought I was being all tactful, and what does lover-boy do? He falls asleep!' she said. 'And you'll need to go now because visitor's hours are over. Give him a nice kiss if you want—I won't look.'

Zina took her at her word and then got up to leave. 'I'll see you in the evening,' she said to Alisha, and the girl nodded.

It felt weird to be so completely accepted by Ishaan's family, Zina realised. Shiven's parents had always disapproved of her, and her own family was still recovering from her unconventional choice of career.

Her phone rang and she looked at the number with a gulp of dismay. Rehaan. He'd definitely sack her this time—she had forgotten she had a job, she hadn't even bothered to call and tell him she wouldn't be coming in.

His voice sounded peculiar though, as if he had just swallowed a frog. 'Are you...' he cleared his throat, and tried again. 'Are you planning to come to work today? Because we have a bit of a...situation here.'

Rehaan refused to tell her more, and Zina jumped into a cab to get to the salon. When she walked in, she got strange looks from Suzy and Dilip and pretty much everyone who worked in the salon. 'Where's Rehaan?' she asked, too worked up to try and figure why they were looking at her as if she had grown a second head. Suzy jerked her head towards Rehaan's office. 'In there.'

He wasn't alone though, Zina realised, a tide of pure fury washing over her as she saw Shiven sitting in the chair opposite Rehaan's desk. His head was buried in his hands and his shoulders were shaking slightly. Rehaan was watching him with the wary expression of a man who found out that he had accidentally let a grizzly bear into his living room.

'What's he doing here?' Zina asked through her teeth. Shiven had been crying, she realised, and somehow that made her even angrier.

'He wanted to buy the salon as a peace offering for you,' Rehaan said in a totally expressionless voice.

'I can't believe this...' Shiven looked up and started to say, 'Zina, I'm so sorry...' but he didn't get to finish the sentence. Zina had whipped around and located Rehaan's case of tools—there were a pair of scissors there, so sharp that even touching the blade drew blood! In the next instant, the scissors were against Shiven's throat. 'I'm going to kill you,' she hissed, white-hot rage pulsing through her veins. 'You complete animal, I can't believe you touched Ishaan...'

Shiven said nothing. His large eyes looking into hers with an expression that suggested a wounded animal more than anything else.

'Zina, if you're going to kill anyone, I'd rather like it if you took them out of my premises first,' Rehaan said carefully. 'And just a thought, maybe talking it through would help?'

Zina threw a contemptuous glance over her shoulder. 'My boyfriend's in hospital because of this creep, Rehaan. Ishaan almost died! I don't think I want to talk this one through, thank you very much!' Her voice shook, and Rehaan sat back quietly in his chair, a thoughtful expression on his face.

'I didn't realise...' Shiven's voice was a dull croak, but Zina didn't let up.

'Didn't realise what? That if you hit a man half your size and half your age, you'd probably injure him badly? I suppose you expect me to be grateful you didn't half-kill me as well while you were at it?'

Shiven gave a strangled moan of protest, and Zina's shoulders suddenly slumped, and she stepped away from him.

'I should never have gotten involved with you,' she said. 'It's the biggest mistake I ever made in my life, and unfortunately, it's Ishaan who's paying the price.'

'I'm moving back to Delhi,' Shiven said, putting a hesitant hand out towards her. He realised only after Ishaan's uncle spoke to him that he had made a terrible mistake. All this while he thought he was protecting Zina from being hurt, and in the process he had almost killed a man and ruined his own career. And worst of all, there was disgust and naked hate in Zina's eyes when she looked at him.

'Perhaps that's the best thing you could do,' she said tiredly. 'Just stay away from me and everyone I know, Shiven.'

'I'll see you out,' Rehaan said, standing up. 'Give me those scissors, Zina.' She handed them to him and didn't look up as Rehaan ushered Shiven out of the room.

'He's gone,' Rehaan said, coming back into the room a few minutes later.

'I'm sorry,' Zina said, feeling too tired even to cry. 'I've made an utter mess of my life, and I've dragged everyone I know into it. It's okay if you want to sack me. I don't really care anymore.'

'Well, I care,' Rehaan said. 'The producer of the show called me a couple of hours ago. Apparently they've been through the test sequences we shot last week, and they want to increase your role in the show. If I sack you, I'll have to go around hunting for another whack-job like you who can cut hair and mouth off to the cameras.'

Zina looked up at him, hope dawning in her eyes. 'You serious?' she asked, and as he nodded, she launched herself across the room at him. 'Rehaan, you're the best! Love you!'

'Umpphh,' Rehaan said as he tried to fend her off. 'Thanks, but I'm a married man, and I've seen what happens to your boyfriends. Take the rest of the day off, but be back at work at seven tomorrow—that's when we start shooting.'

※

Dear Nanaji,

I told you about Zina—she's a friend of Papa's and she takes Hindi lessons from Mom. She's going to be on TV in a new reality show.

I read the books you told me about and I liked them. Everyone in my class is reading either Percy Jackson or the Hunger Games series. I don't really like either, but I had to read them to know what everyone is talking about.

It's getting a little boring here—can't you come down for a visit? There was something I wanted to tell you, but I can't say it on e-mail.

Love,
Gayatri

nine

'I CAN'T GO to school,' Gayatri said. 'I don't feel well, and everybody hates me anyway.'

'Everyone doesn't hate you, baby,' Anjali said patiently, wondering if all kids this age were so self-centred. Gayatri hadn't asked once how Ishaan was, though Zina talked about him all the time.

'Well, I'm not going,' Gayatri said, her expression mulish. 'You can't force me to go.'

'Oh can't I?' Anjali was fast losing her temper. 'Get off the bed and go get ready right now if you don't want me to give you a hard slap!'

Gayatri got up and went into the bathroom without a word. 'Come and have breakfast once you've bathed and changed,' Anjali called out, feeling a little ashamed of having lost her temper.

Ten minutes later when Gayatri came out of the bathroom, her face was pale. 'I think I got my period,' she faltered out. 'There's blood all over my shorts.'

Of course she didn't have to go to school after that—twelve was a little early to have her first period, but Anjali wasn't too surprised. Gayatri had matured physically over the last couple of months, and her recent mood swings were probably a symptom of the early onset of puberty. In a way, Anjali felt relieved—her daughter hadn't turned into a monster, she had just been growing up, and Anjali had been too stupid to recognise the signs.

She got the girl fixed up with a sanitary napkin, and tucked her into bed with a hot water bottle. 'Try and rest a bit,' she said. 'I'll call your teacher and tell her you won't be coming to school today.' The school had instructed parents to let the class teacher know when a girl started menstruating so that they could be handled a little more sensitively.

Gayatri groaned and turned her head to the wall. The cramps were really terrible, and she hadn't realised how *gross* the whole thing was. It didn't feel like she had grown up or anything, it felt like she had some kind of a loathsome disease. There were other girls in the class who'd started menstruating, and if everything was normal Gayatri would have waited till school was over and called one of them. But now, they'd probably not want to talk to her...

Anjali came into the room a few times to check on her, but Gayatri pretended to be asleep every time. Her brain was whirring in her head like a windmill as she tried to figure out what to do. Today's reprieve had been a godsend, but on Monday, her mother would expect her to go back to school, and she'd rather die first. Her father was out of town on work, and she couldn't appeal to him either. The more she thought about it, the more she felt that there was only one solution—go back to Indore to her grandfather. She could buy a train ticket and catch a train tomorrow and she'd be with Nanaji by Sunday morning. And once she was there, she could convince Nanaji to let her live with him and go back to her old school.

Booking the ticket online with her mother's debit card was easy—after she had forgotten her PIN and passwords a few times, Anjali had taken to writing them down in a diary that she kept on her desk. Gayatri just had to enter her own mobile number and e-mail id into the booking website, and she made sure she did the booking when her mother was in the bathroom. Her mom's phone pinged as the debit card was charged, and she grabbed it and deleted the message that had come in from the bank confirming the transaction. Easy-peasy. Now all she needed to do was pack a small bag and sneak out of the house when her mother was away.

Tiwari was chatting happily with a security guard when Gayatri went downstairs, and he leapt to his feet when he saw her. *'Kahin jaana hai, Gayatri?'* he asked, and Gayatri hesitated. Tiwari wasn't the sharpest knife in the drawer, but it was likely that he'd be suspicious if he saw her walking out of the complex alone.

'I need to go to my friend's place,' she said. 'It's

opposite Mumbai Central.'

'That big building,' Tiwari nodded knowledgeably. 'Great Eastern.'

'Yes,' Gayatri said. Great Eastern was close enough, and she'd make sure Tiwari dropped her at the main gate.

'*Andar nahin jaana?*' he asked, and she shook her head. 'No, my friend will be out in a minute. We're going for a birthday party, and her mom will drop me back. *Aap ghar chale jao.*'

She waited till he was out of sight and then doubled back to cross the road to the station. She had purposely dressed in a kurti over jeans and tied her hair into a ponytail. With her height, it was easy to pass off as being older than she really was—in the ticket she had put her age down as seventeen. A little work with a pen and eraser on her old Indore school identity card had changed her age there as well, and now all she needed to do was get on the train unnoticed.

The station was crowded, and she needed to ask a few people before she found the platform. After that, she just had to wait for half an hour till the train chugged into the station.

Anjali got home at eight o'clock. She had taken Daffy, Erik and Bill to watch the new animated version of the 'Mahabharata', and had had to translate in whispers all through.

'Come up, and I'll give you the book I promised you,'

she said to Daffy who was dropping her home on her way back to her working women's hostel in Colaba. Zina was already home, tired but exhilarated after a day's shooting. Ishaan was going to be discharged from the hospital on Monday, and she couldn't wait.

'She really seems to be in love,' Daffy said in wonder when Zina went in to freshen up. 'It's like she's changed into a completely different person.'

'Let's hope it lasts,' Anjali said drily. 'Hang on now, where's that book?' She hunted around in the living room bookshelf, and then called out to Gayatri.

'Gayatri baahar gayi hai,' Lalita said appearing at the living room door. 'Tiwari said she's coming back with a friend from some birthday party.'

Anjali frowned. Granted the Wellington kids seemed to have more birthday parties than normal human beings, but she was pretty sure there wasn't one today. 'Did she go alone?' Anjali asked Lalita.

'Ji didi,' the girl said nervously. 'She just told me she was going downstairs to the garden, Tiwari told me later about the party.'

'Wait till I get my hands on her,' Anjali muttered, dialling Gayatri's number. 'The number you're trying to reach is currently unavailable,' the recorded message said.

Breathe, don't panic, Anjali told herself, as she called Devika. 'No, Gayatri's not here,' Devika said, sounding puzzled. 'And as far as I know there's no party today. Unless one of the boys is holding one and Rhea isn't invited.'

Anjali tried Shaan next, and with rising panic, each child in Gayatri's class, but the answer was the same. No party. No, Gayatri's not here. No, I've not spoken to her today.

'Tell Tiwari to come upstairs,' she told Lalita, beginning to pace. Zina and Daffy were watching her with worried expressions, but she was too keyed up to talk to them.

'Mumbai Central ke saamne,' Tiwari said, sounding bewildered. 'She told me not to wait.'

'She doesn't have a friend at Great Eastern,' Anjali snapped. The fear was building up now, and she looked at Tiwari with suspicion.

Zina came out of Gayatri's room carrying an envelope. 'She seems to have left a note,' she said. 'This was on her desk.'

The note said, *'Dear Mom,*

'I don't want to go back to school on Monday, so I'm going to Nanaji. Don't worry, I've booked a ticket in the reserve compartment and everything—I'll be fine. I'll call you when I get there.

Gayatri'

Anjali crushed the note between her fingers, so angry that she could hardly speak. 'Tiwari, gaadi nikaalo,' she said.

'*Ji madam*,' Tiwari said, scuttling away like a crab in a hurry.

'But where are you going?' Zina asked. 'You can't rush off like that, the train would already have left.'

'There's a chance it hasn't,' Anjali said through gritted

teeth. 'And if it has, I'll catch the next train or bus or plane or whatever and go after her.'

'I'll come with you,' Daffy said, and as Zina raised her eyebrows, 'To the station at least.'

They all went finally, piling into the car with a nervous Tiwari at the wheel. 'There's only one train to Indore from Mumbai Central and it was supposed to leave at 7.30 pm,' Zina said scanning the railway timetable on her phone.

'Maybe it got delayed,' Daffy said hopefully. 'These trains keep getting cancelled and rescheduled.'

But it hadn't been cancelled or rescheduled, a porter told them. It had left exactly on time. 'They're always reforming the wrong things,' Daffy said bitterly. 'Now the trains are on time, next thing we know, people will actually start following traffic rules.'

'Stop babbling, Daffy,' Zina said. 'Let's go find the Station Master, shall we? He should have a reservations chart—we can check if Gayatri's name is on it.'

'Wow, that's actually a good idea,' Daffy said, looking impressed. So far, she thought of Zina as being strictly decorative—it was a revelation seeing that she had a fully-functional brain.

'Anjali madam!' Anjali turned to see one of her former Chemistry students hurrying towards her, resplendent in an Indian Railways uniform.

'Namaste, Vivek,' she said.

Vivek swooped down and touched Anjali's feet. 'Jeete

raho, beta,' Anjali muttered, bravely resisting the impulse to yelp and jump away. Not only was he embarrassing her, she was worried that he'd get a glimpse of her panties when he straightened up. She wore a short dress for the movie and afterwards, she had been in too much of a hurry to think about changing. The whole guru-shishya thing didn't really go with Western clothes.

'I'm with the Railways now,' Vivek informed her proudly, as if his uniform wasn't signalling the fact loudly enough.

'Great, so you can help us,' Zina said, pushing forward. 'We need to find out if Anjali madam's daughter took a train to Indore from here.'

After Vivek had finished goggling at Zina's film-star looks, he actually turned out to be quite helpful, digging out the reservations chart and confirming that Gayatri's name was on it.

'Is there any way you can find out if she's actually on the train?' Daffy asked, not thinking he'd say yes. But he nodded immediately, looking very pleased with himself. 'I have ticket-checkers on board, I can call them and ask them to check. Only...' he frowned a little. 'If she knows that you know she's on that train, will she try to get off before Indore or something?'

It was a complicated sentence, but all three women understood what he meant. Anjali bit her lip. 'Maybe,' she said. 'Can you tell the ticket-checker not to alarm her?'

'Ma'am, if you can WhatsApp me her picture, I can

send it to the ticket-checker, and he won't even need to speak to her.'

'You can't let him send Gayatri's picture to some strange guy,' Daffy said in an undertone.

'She's all alone with a train full of strange guys,' Zina retorted. 'One picture isn't going to make things worse.'

Anjali had to agree with her, and in another ten minutes, the WhatsApping ticket-checker confirmed that Gayatri indeed was on the train. Anjali's shoulders sagged in relief. 'Wait till I get my hands on that little brat,' she muttered. 'She'll wish she had never seen a train in her life.' She tried Gayatri's number again, but it was still switched off.

'When's the next train to Indore, Vivek?' Zina asked, but Daffy clucked impatiently. 'It'll take ages to get there by train. Isn't there a night flight?'

Vivek shook his head. 'The first flight is in the morning,' he said. 'My brother-in-law always takes it when he needs to go, even though I offer to book him a first-class ticket on the train.' He ruminated sadly for few seconds on his brother-in-law's unreasonable prejudice against the Railways, and then brightened up.

'But if you take the morning flight you'll still reach before the train,' he said.

'So let's do it then,' Anjali said. 'Thanks, Vivek, I really appreciate it. And once Gayatri's back home, you must come over for dinner. We live just down the road at Mahalakshmi.'

'You made his day,' Daffy remarked as they got into the car. 'He'll be telling his family for years how he helped track down your daughter.'

'Oh hell,' said Anjali. 'I need to call my Dad. Vivek will also probably tell the whole of Indore that Gayatri's run away. I give the news twenty minutes to reach my Dad.'

'What if you tell him to keep his mouth shut?' Daffy asked, and Zina gave her a pitying glance. 'It doesn't work that way,' she said. 'Better for Anjali to call her Dad, and then go home and book her ticket to Indore.'

Anjali shut her eyes as soon as she got onto the flight. She had had a largely sleepless night, and right now all she wanted to do, was think of exactly what she'd say when she saw Gayatri. The temptation to walk up to her and give her a hard slap was huge, and her palm was actually tingling with anticipation. It wouldn't work though. In spite of her very justifiable anger, Anjali knew that she needed to build bridges with her daughter rather than push her away.

At some point during the short flight she fell asleep, waking up with a start when the plane landed. People around her were standing up and trying to get their luggage out of the overhead bins in spite of multiple announcements asking them to stay seated until the plane came to a complete halt. One particularly enthusiastic man managed to step on her toes thrice and Anjali couldn't help hoping that he'd get hit on the head with a suitcase.

Her father was waiting outside the airport in his trusted old Fiat. 'We have just about enough time to get to the station,' he said grumpily, but Anjali knew he was quite as worried as she was. 'Should I drive?' she asked and he gave her his special glare, the one he usually reserved for queue-jumpers and door-to-door salesmen.

'I'm perfectly capable of driving,' he said, and Anjali gave him an apologetic hug. 'Come on then,' she said. 'Let's go and meet that granddaughter of yours.'

ten

'SHE MANAGED TO reach the railway station just before Gayatri's train pulled in,' Daffy told Erik on the phone. 'Poor kid, she must have been completely gobsmacked.'

Erik frowned. 'Where do you pick up words like that?' he asked. 'I've never heard a real person say "gobsmacked".'

'It's a Bengali thing,' Daffy explained. 'When you're growing up you're made to read every book written in the UK from the nineteenth and twentieth century, and you're supposed to use at least one long word from them in every sentence you speak.'

'I have a feeling that telling tall stories is a Ben-gaar-lee thing as well,' Erik said. 'Because every time I catch you doing something weird, you say it's a Ben-gaar-lee thing.'

'That's coz Bengalis are weird,' Daffy said, flushing slightly. 'Anyway, I'd only called to tell you that everything's okay, and Anjali will be back on Friday. Only she's bringing her Dad back with her, so I'm not sure if the Saturday class is on.'

'It's on,' Erik said. 'She messaged me.' He hesitated a little. 'Daffy, are you doing something for dinner tonight?'

'Yes, I'm eating it,' Daffy said crossly. Erik had transferred his attentions from Zina to her more than a month back, but he was appallingly slow. Even a two-toed sloth would have managed to ask her out by now.

'No, I mean, would you like to have dinner with me? The rooftop bar at the Four Seasons is supposed to be pretty good.'

'Yes, sure,' Daffy said as casually as she could.

Zina raised her eyebrows as she put the phone down. 'Finally?' she asked, and Daffy said, 'Finally. Though it'll probably take him a year or so to actually kiss me or anything.'

'You like him, don't you?'

Daffy nodded. 'But if you tell him, I'll make sure you get turfed out of the hostel before you can say "Ishaan Mehta".'

The room next to Daffy's in the working women's hostel had fallen vacant unexpectedly, and Zina had managed to bag it, which took care of her housing issue, but created a whole host of new and interesting problems for Daffy. Like having to take messages for Zina at odd hours because Zina couldn't be bothered to charge her phone. And Zina indiscriminately 'borrowing' lipsticks, stoles and shoes and forgetting to return them. Still, life was definitely a lot more exciting with her around.

'Are you shooting for the show today?' Daffy asked curiously. Zina shook her head. 'No, they're editing the first few episodes now and they'll restart shooting on Thursday. Ishaan's coming out of hospital today.'

For all her usual lack of discretion, Zina didn't talk about Ishaan much, and Daffy hesitated a little before she asked, 'Are you going to his house?'

Zina nodded. 'He needs to stay home and rest for a week or so,' she said, and Daffy noticed that she was crossing her fingers behind her back. 'I thought I'd go around and cheer him up a bit. Do I look okay?'

Daffy surveyed the dashing picture Zina made in a pair of skin-tight red jeggings and a white sleeveless, nearly see-through chiffon top that clearly showed the outline of her pert little breasts. Her flyaway hair hung loose around her shoulders in loose waves, and her eyes were outlined with kohl to make them look even larger than usual.

'You look great,' Daffy said honestly. 'Only, is his mom going to be around? Because if she is, she might think you're a bad influence on her little boy.'

One of the nice things about Zina was that you could say pretty much anything to her without offending her. She laughed, making her dangling earrings jiggle. 'I don't think she is,' she said. 'And even if she is, I'm sure I can convince her that her little boy deserves a treat after all he's been through!'

As it turned out, Dr Suhasini wasn't at home. Alisha opened the door and gave Zina a knowing look. 'Ishaan's in his room,' she said. And as Zina headed towards the room, she added warningly, 'He's supposed to be in bed.'

Zina felt like retorting that everything she'd like to do with Ishaan could be done perfectly well in bed, but she bit the words back. Wouldn't do having Alisha go running back to her mom with a complaint. She knocked on the door lightly and then pushed it open.

Ishaan was standing by the window. He was wearing a thin black T-shirt and loose drawstring linen trousers. He had lost weight while he was in hospital—his perfectly sculpted cheekbones were standing out a little more than usual, and his face was drawn. His hair was longer as well, flopping untidily over his forehead. Only his eyes were just the same, and they blazed with happiness as he saw Zina. Being Ishaan though, he didn't do the conventional boyfriend thing and hold his arms out to her. Instead, he leaned back against the window and said easily, 'Did Christmas come early?'

'What?'

'The Santa Claus get-up,' he said, gesturing towards her white top and red stole and jeggings. 'Not that I'm complaining, you're exactly what I'd like to find under my Christmas tree.'

Zina crossed the room and put her hands on his shoulders. 'You talk way too much,' she said, leaning in and kissing him on the lips. He tasted amazing, like cinnamon and honey, and she had to exercise considerable self-control not to drag him to the bed and have her way with him.

Instead she drew away and smiled at him slightly. 'How are you?' she asked softly.

'Surviving,' he said, his eyes dancing wickedly. 'I need lots—and I mean lots—of tender loving care.' His hands were roving under the chiffon top now, leaving her in no doubt as to the kind of care he needed. Instinctively, Zina reached for him, drawing back as she felt him flinch.

'Aren't you...'

'About to die of frustration?' his expression was wry as he kissed the nape of her neck. 'Yes. And you're right, I can't do much more than kiss you until I recover fully.'

'Don't get him over-excited,' a disapproving voice said from the door. 'He's supposed to be resting.'

'Go away, Ally,' Ishaan instructed without looking up.

'Shan't. It's time for your soup and your medicines.'

Ishaan groaned and removed his hands from Zina's waist. 'Meet Florence Nightingale,' he said to her, waving towards Alisha. 'Earlier known as my baby sister.'

'I think she's quite right,' Zina said, stepping regretfully but decisively away from Ishaan. 'Come and sit with us, Alisha.'

'Unless you have more interesting things to do,' Ishaan murmured, but he clearly didn't mean it because he reached across and ruffled Alisha's hair.

'Soup,' she said firmly and handed him a mug. 'I went downstairs and got some fresh oregano to put in it, so it should be nicer than yesterday's.'

Zina tried to imagine one of her own sisters doing something like that for her and failed. Maybe if she were actually dying or something—or no, not even then. She had always been the cuckoo in the crow's nest, and the rest of her family hadn't known how to deal with her. Pushing the thought to a corner of her brain, she smiled at Alisha. 'No school today?'

'It's Saturday,' Alisha said patiently. 'School's shut.'

'I used to have school on Saturdays,' Zina said. She had gone to a small convent school near Bangalore, and every day had been sheer torture. 'But now that you say it, I remember Gayatri having a holiday last Saturday.'

'Thought she ran away last Saturday,' Alisha said, and Ishaan's eyebrows flew up. 'Gayatri ran away?' he asked 'Where to?'

'To her grandfather in Indore,' Zina said. 'She apparently had some adjustment issues at school, and after this last episode, she didn't want to go back.'

'Last episode of what?' Ishaan asked. 'The Mahabharata?'

Both Zina and Alisha clucked at him exasperatedly. 'Honestly, sometimes you're just weird,' Alisha said. 'She ran away and left you on the floor here, don't you remember?'

Ishaan looked frankly puzzled now. 'Of course I

remember, what does that have to do with her not wanting to go to school? Or running away from home?'

There was an awkward pause. Zina knew about the call Alisha had made to Gayatri, but for the first time in a long career of focussed tactlessness she consciously kept her mouth zipped. Alisha finally spoke.

'I called and told her that I'd make life difficult for her at school,' she said defiantly. 'And I don't care if you tell mom or if Gayatri reports me for bullying. I hope she stays in Indore and never comes back. I completely hate her!'

'She's feeling pretty bad about what she did,' Zina murmured, feeling duty-bound to put in a word.

'She *should* feel bad,' Alisha said resentfully. 'She's either a complete coward or an absolutely cold-hearted little bitch. What kind of girl leaves an injured person on the floor and runs away?'

'Not your kind perhaps,' Ishaan said, putting an arm around Alisha and walking her to the window. 'Think of it from Gayatri's point of view,' he suggested. 'She was already scared because she was about to meet you and let's face it, you're pretty scary.' Alisha giggled involuntarily.

'Then this big King Kong of a guy barged in and beat me up. There was no one else in the flat, and I was in no shape to protect her. She didn't know if the guy was coming back. Wouldn't running away be the natural reaction?'

'She could have locked the door and called someone,' Alisha said.

'I don't think she was in a state to think logically, Ally,' Ishaan said. 'She called someone as soon as she could. And there was no way she could have known that I was badly hurt.'

Alisha chewed her lip and looked thoughtful. 'So what d'you want me to do?' she asked finally.

'Cut her some slack,' he said. 'From what Zina says, she's had a tough time adjusting to Wellington.'

'She's brought it upon herself, making bitchy remarks about people,' Alisha muttered. 'Now that she's run away to Indore, I think she should just stay there and not come back.'

'Really?' Ishaan said, and the steely note in his voice made Alisha flinch. 'Ally, you're a born leader, but you need to understand that it'll take very little for you to tip over and become a bully. And that's not the kind of person I want my sister to be. I can understand why you were upset with Gayatri, but it's over now. Grow up and move on, and make sure you give the girl a chance.'

'Okay,' Alisha said in a very subdued voice. Ishaan tapped her cheek lightly. 'Off you go now,' he said. 'Love you.'

'Love you too,' Alisha said, turning around to press her face against his shoulder for an instant. 'I'll be nice to her, but only because you're telling me to.' She ran out of the room, and Zina said, 'Wow. Well done.'

Ishaan sagged against the nearest wall in mock-exhaustion.

'You think? This has taken years of my life! For pity's sake, go latch the door and come here. I desperately need some cheering up!'

Zina obediently latched the door, and came to stand in front of him, her eyes sparkling with mischief. 'I know just what you need,' she said, reaching out for him.

eleven

'STOP *FUSSING!*' GAYATRI said crossly. She was leaving for a school educational tour to Goa, and Anjali was driving her crazy with last minute advice and packing tips. 'I told you, I'm not allowed to carry a phone. And there's no point packing a first-aid kit, Miss Kumar is carrying a humongous box full of bandages and Betadine and stuff.'

'Maybe you should carry snow-shoes,' Sushil said solemnly as he entered the room and surveyed the things strewn around the open suitcase. 'And a hammer. And perhaps a washing machine and a couple of kilos of chocolate.'

'I'll take the chocolate,' Gayatri said promptly as Anjali glared at him. 'If you think I'm going over the top, you should look at the messages on the class WhatsApp group,' she said. 'Some of the mothers are going completely ballistic.'

'So are you,' Gayatri informed her kindly. 'Chill mom, I'll be fine.'

Anjali hesitated a bit. 'Is everything all right between you and Rhea and the other girls?' It was only after Gayatri ran away that Anjali had figured out quite how bad it had been for her at school. Now that Alisha was on Gayatri's side, things were better, but Anjali couldn't stop worrying.

Gayatri nodded. 'All good,' she said. 'Especially the girls in my house, ever since they figured out I'm brilliant at sports.' Grinning happily, she added, 'If they annoy me, I'll pretend I sprained my ankle, and there goes their chance of winning the house cup.'

'Okay,' Anjali said faintly, wondering whether she was responsible for the blackmailing gene or Sushil. Sushil probably—he had always known how to get his way.

'It's time to leave,' Sushil reminded them. 'The train leaves in an hour.'

If she had been in any doubt about Gayatri's popularity, she was proved wrong the minute they set foot on the railway platform. Gayatri joined Rhea and a bunch of other friends on the platform, and while she was not the centre of attention, she was definitely as well accepted as Rhea.

'Some of us are catching up for a drink once the train leaves,' one of the mothers said to Anjali. 'You guys want to join?'

'Would have loved to, but we've already made plans,' Sushil said, putting an arm around Anjali's shoulders.

'Have we?' Anjali mouthed at him, and he grinned. 'Say goodbye to Gayatri,' he said. 'And try not to burst into tears and embarrass her hideously.' He had a point—

Anjali had never been separated from her daughter before, and she was feeling distinctly weepy. Still she smiled and waved as the train pulled out of the station.

'I've booked a table at the Taj for dinner,' Sushil said when the train was finally out of sight. 'D'you realise, this is the first time we've been properly alone together since Gayatri was born? Not counting the time I was in hospital getting my tonsils removed.'

'Definitely not counting that,' Anjali said, shuddering at the memory. 'You were the worst patient ever.' She slipped her arm through his as they walked out of the station—the week that Gayatri was away had taken on a sudden appeal.

Dinner was wonderful, and Anjali realised that she was actually feeling relaxed after a long, long while. Partly because of the wine, but mainly because Sushil was making a genuine effort to connect with her. He talked about their college days, and about her work, and what she wanted to do with her life other than just be Gayatri's mom.

'This was like old days,' she said as they walked out of the hotel. 'I'd forgotten how much we used to talk to each other.'

'And argue,' Sushil said. 'Don't forget that.'

'And argue,' she agreed. 'About totally silly stuff sometimes.'

'Not planning to argue with me today, are you?' he asked, his voice low and excitingly sexy. 'Because I can think of a lot more exciting things to do when we get home.'

They were waiting for the driver to get the car when a woman dressed in a sari walked past. She looked at Anjali, hesitated for a second, and then turned back. 'Hi Anjali!' she said, a wide smile on her face. Anjali stared at her blankly for bit—the woman was in her twenties, and heavily made up, and Anjali had absolutely no clue who she was. 'We met when I came over to your place a couple of weeks ago,' the woman prompted. 'I'm Anil's relationship manager from the bank. We discussed the investments you guys should make over the next few months...'

Oh God, Anjali thought. This was like one of those moments in a movie when you looked at the heroine and wondered exactly how stupid she was to have got into a situation like this. Anil and she had laughed about the girl going back and drawing up an investment plan for the two of them. Why-oh-why hadn't they had the sense to tell her that they weren't married?

Sushil was frowning. 'Anil's place?' he said, and the woman finally registered that he and Anjali were together. 'Yes,' she said, looking up at him uncertainly. 'This is my husband, Sushil,' Anjali said. 'I'm Shefali,' the woman said, holding out her hand. 'I'm so sorry, I seem to have got a little mixed up...'

No you haven't, Anjali felt like saying. From the way Shefali's eyes were moving between the two of them, it was clear that she knew she had put her foot in it, and was trying to extract the maximum possible entertainment from the situation.

'Shefali works in Anil's bank,' Anjali said. 'I happened to be visiting him when she came over to discuss his portfolio.'

'Right,' Sushil said. 'Our car's here. See you, Shefali.'

There was complete silence in the car for the next few minutes. Anjali had a mad urge to giggle—the whole situation was so utterlly ridiculous. 'I didn't know you'd ever visited Anil,' Sushil said carefully after a bit.

'He missed a couple of classes,' Anjali said. 'I was in the area, waiting for Gayatri's gym class to get over, and we ran into each other at a book store. It made sense to go to his place and help him catch up.'

'It didn't occur to either of you to correct this girl when she thought you were married to Anil?'

Anjali sighed. 'She was hitting on him, asking him for meetings every few days, and calling him repeatedly. At the time it seemed like a good idea, letting her think we were in a relationship.'

'Does Nair think the same?' Sushil asked, a distinct edge to his voice. 'That you're in a relationship? Like Deven Khatri did?'

'Can we postpone this till we get home?' Anjali said, no longer wanting to giggle. Sushil was behaving as if he had caught her making out with Anil on Marine Drive. On live TV. She nodded her head towards the driver. 'I don't really want to talk when we have an audience.'

The rest of the drive was completed in silence, and

when they got home, Sushil said, 'You go on upstairs. I need to settle something about the parking.'

'You said you went there only once,' Sushil said without preamble when he came into the flat a few minutes later. 'Tiwari tells me you used to go there every week, whenever Gayatri had a gym class.'

Anjali turned to stare at him. 'You asked Tiwari,' she said slowly, anger beginning to stir within her. 'When did I tell you I went there just once? And how *dare* you check on me with Tiwari? And who're you to comment on whom I should visit and whom I shouldn't? You're the one who had an affair while we were still married! You're the one who had Zina staying in your flat! What *right* do you have to quiz me about what I'm doing?' She stopped for breath, her chest heaving, and glared at him.

'I never lied to you!' Sushil said furiously. 'You wouldn't even have *known* if I hadn't told you!'

'Oh, so that makes it okay, does it?' Anjali said, practically spitting the words out. 'So if I'd decided to have sex with Anil it would have been okay if I'd just *told* you, right? You'd have given me your blessings.'

'Did you?' Sushil asked. 'If you've actually been sleeping with that...that...I swear I'll...'

'You'll invite him to your exclusive club of people who sleep around?' Anjali said. 'That's so sweet.' As Sushil gaped at her, she marched into their bedroom, and picked up a T-shirt and a pair of tracks from the shelf where Sushil kept his nightwear. 'Here,' she said, tossing them at him. 'It'd be nice if you moved to the spare room. Just for the record, nothing happened with Anil. But I wish it had.' With that, she slammed the door, locked it, and plonked down on the bed still fuming. She was angry about so many different things that it was difficult to sort them out in her head. Sushil's double-standards. His checking with Tiwari on her, his accusing her of lying. 'How dare he?' was pretty much the dominant theme running through her mind, and she finally relieved her pent-up anger by picking up a book and hurling it across the room. It hit a lamp which promptly fell over with a satisfying clunk.

'Damn, damn, damn Shefali,' Anjali said out loud. She was still furious with Sushil, but smashing the lamp had calmed her down a bit. Plus she was feeling rather regretful about the ruined evening. If it hadn't been for Shefali opening her stupid mouth, she'd have been in bed with Sushil right now, having fabulous sex. Oh well, there was nothing she could do about it now.

'You're going to Chicago to study organisational behaviour?' Zina asked. 'What's wrong with doing a nice MSc, Psychology in a Gujju college in Mumbai?'

'It's not the same thing,' Ishaan said, pressing her hand gently, his lean fingers interlaced with hers. 'I'm sort of aiming to be India's next Amartya Sen.'

'Ah that,' Zina said nodding knowledgeably, though she had no clue what he was talking about. All she had managed to gather was that he was going away, and the thought was breaking her heart—it took all her self-control and then some to keep a light smile on her face. Her head was in a whirl. Did this mean he was dumping her? Zina had always been the one to do the dumping, and while she liked new experiences she wasn't at all sure whether being dumped before breakfast by a boy six years younger was the kind of new experience she wanted to have.

'When do you leave?'

'In a month,' Ishaan said, and pushed his fingers through his unruly hair, his mouth twisting down at the corners. 'I'll miss you,' he said abruptly.

Zina gave him a quick smile. 'You'll find a *gori* girlfriend soon enough.'

'While you go around hooking up with completely unsuitable men,' Ishaan said, not fooled for a minute by her apparent calm. 'There'll be no one around to keep you out of trouble.'

'Well, as far as being unsuitable goes...' Zina began to say, but she was cut off by his mouth descending fiercely on hers. 'I decide whether I'm suitable for you or not,' he said, once she was completely breathless with lust and clinging to his lean body for support. 'And going by your current state, I think I'm as suitable as suitable gets.'

'Not fair,' Zina protested after submitting to being kissed thoroughly. 'First you tell me you're leaving, then you try to make me feel bad about it.' She was still trying to keep a jokey tone going, but her voice had a distinct wobble in it. 'It's not like you won't go if I throw myself at you and say *"tussi naa jao"*.'

'Try it and see,' Ishaan said, and she yanked herself out of his arms. 'Thanks, but I'm not the type to make a fool of myself over a man. It was good while it lasted, kid.' Zina might kid herself into thinking she sounded as tough as an old boot, but as usual, Ishaan's eyes saw too much.

'I'd stay if I could,' he said softly. 'You know I would. But this college is very tough to get into—it's a brilliant chance, I can't thow it away.'

'I'm not asking you to.'

'I'm still tempted.' Ishaan's eyes looked sadder and a lot older. 'We have something that's...strong. It's been there right since I first saw you with that ridiculous bunch of bankers. If I'd met you just a few years later...'

'You'd have asked me to marry you and have your babies,' Zina said tartly. 'Look, there's no point agonising about it. We have a month and let's make the most of it. *Kal kisne dekha hai.*'

'I need to compliment Anjali on your Hindi,' Ishaan murmured, but he was smiling. 'Sure, let's make the most of this month.'

Making the most of the month seemed to involve an awful lot of alcohol, Zina thought to herself a couple of weeks later. This was the third night in a row that she had woken up with a hangover. She couldn't even blame Ishaan for it, because he hardly drank anything. The previous night in particular was completely her own fault—she downed one tequila shot after another, and snapped at Ishaan when he suggested that she was overdoing it. Pity she hadn't listened to him. Her head throbbed as if a million tiny sledgehammers were pounding away inside it. Carefully, she opened one eye and surveyed her surroundings. Ishaan had borrowed a cottage in Alibag from a friend, and they'd stayed there overnight. 'Cottage' was actually a bit of an understatement—the place was lavish, and even the bathrooms were bigger than her room in the women's hostel.

'Feeling better?'

Zina opened the other eye and gave Ishaan a baleful look. 'My poor brain is still trying to recover from all the heavy talk yesterday.'

A bunch of Ishaan's friends had come over the previous night, and the conversation had been depressingly highbrow. Oh, they'd laughed and joked like any other college kids, but there had been long discussions about global warming and tribal art, and one boy had even started off on third world debt. Zina had a sneaking suspicion that they thought she was a bit of an airhead. After a while, she only concentrated on the tequila shots and played games on her phone when no one was looking.

'I'm sorry,' Ishaan said, coming to sit on the bed next to her. 'I've been avoiding these guys for a bit, but we were really close growing up. This was probably the last chance we had to meet as a group. Most of us will be moving out of Mumbai soon.'

'No worries, they were fun,' Zina said, lying through her teeth. Her heart twisted as she looked at Ishaan. He was so incredibly handsome with his hair flopping anyhow on his forehead, and his dark eyes full of concern that she wanted to pull him into her arms and never let him go. Instead, she sat up and shifted imperceptibly away from him. 'I guess I drank too much—I've got a terrible headache. What are we doing today?'

'There's a decent spa at the Radisson—d'you want to go there?' Ishaan asked. 'My treat. Maybe it'll help with the hangover.'

For a completely unreasonable second, Zina wanted to snap at him. Sometimes Ishaan treated her like she was a high-maintenance trophy girlfriend, and it bothered her no end.

'No, I don't,' she said. 'Ishaan, could we go back to Mumbai? I need to help Rehaan with some stuff for the show.'

'Okaaay,' he said slowly. 'But hadn't you taken the week off?'

'I had,' Zina said, twisting a corner of the bedsheet between her fingers. 'Only, Ishaan, this isn't working, is it? I feel like I'm saying goodbye to you every minute of the day, and it's getting to me. Maybe a clean break would be better.'

It was only when she saw that he was seriously considering it that she realised that a clean break was the last thing she wanted. She had wanted him to protest, say that he'd spend every minute he had with her before he left for the US. Only there seemed about as much chance of his doing that as of offering not to go at all. Not for the first time in her life, Zina wished she had had the sense to keep her mouth shut.

Ishaan ran a hand through his hair. 'You're right,' he said finally. 'And once I leave for the US, it'll be worse. I don't believe in long-distance relationships.'

For a second, Zina felt slightly sick. She had gotten bored of and dumped six boyfriends in as many years—this was the first time she actually wanted to hang on to a guy, and here he was, saying he didn't believe in long-distance relationships. She bit her lip. Not being with Ishaan any more, not being able to reach out and run her fingers over his smooth, tanned skin, not seeing his eyes crinkle up at the corners when he laughed. The thought was almost unendurable—the only thing that would be worse was his figuring out how she felt.

'Let's get back to Mumbai today then,' Zina said, surprised at how calm and reasonable she sounded. 'You can spend some more time with your family, and I can get back to work.'

'Okay,' Ishaan said, but then he turned and pulled her almost roughly into his arms. 'I'll miss you like crazy,' he murmured into her hair. 'Bloody hell, Zina, why did we have to get the timing so wrong?'

twelve

Three months later

'That has to be the worst haircut I've ever seen,' Zina said in mock horror. 'Dr Kumar, please don't tell me one of your students attacked your hair with a scalpel?'

The motherly looking woman on the screen laughed. She had a jolly laugh that made one think of Govinda movies and Mona Darling jokes. And her hair was frankly terrible—it had been straightened at some point, and the ends were like straw, while at the roots it was dreadfully frizzy and the texture of Scotch Brite. And her current hairstyle made it look as if her hair had been violently attacked by a troupe of very hungry rats.

'I tried out a new beauty parlour near my house' she said, making a rueful face. 'I've not had time to get it fixed since.'

'Hmm... So Rehaan has his job cut out for him,' Zina

said. 'What d'you think Rehaan? Can we fix this, or do we shave her head and send out for a wig?'

'She's good,' Lydia said admiringly. 'She manages to connect with the customer, and she's got this whole jokey thing going with Rehaan. Are they seeing each other?' Anjali's original Hindi class had gathered together to watch the first episode of 'Cut It Out!', and so far, Zina had been brilliant.

'Rehaan's married,' Daffy said. Bill laughed. 'I don't think a minor thing like that would stop Zina if she was really interested,' he said. 'But it's not that kind of chemistry—they look like they're good friends.'

'Where's Zina?' Lydia asked.

'Rehaan and his wife are throwing a party for everyone who works for "Twist",' Anjali said, putting a plate of hummus and pita bread on the table. 'So she's there. They'll be watching this as well, I guess.'

'She's not with that college kid boyfriend of hers anymore?' Erik asked Daffy in an undertone. Erik and Daffy were a proper couple now, and Daffy no longer minded his asking about Zina. 'I'm not sure,' she whispered back. 'He's back in the US now for his studies.'

'Maybe in a year or two, Erik will actually get around to asking that girl to marry him,' Anjali said to Sushil as he came into the kitchen to help her carry out the dinner. 'Daffy's pretty serious about him.'

'Maybe,' Sushil said. 'Though I doubt it. They aren't

big on marriage in Sweden. Haven't you read "The Girl With the Dragon Tattoo"?'

'Haven't you seen what happens to a man who upsets a Bengali woman?' Anjali retorted. 'There's a reason why everyone in Bengal worships Ma Durga.'

'You have a point,' Sushil said. They were back to laughing and joking on the surface, but Sushil didn't seem to trust her any longer. And Anjali hadn't attempted to explain exactly what had happened with Anil. It was partly a pride thing, and partly a resurgence of all the things that had driven them apart in the first place.

'You're looking rather nice today,' Sushil said unexpectedly. Anjali looked up in surprise. 'Umm, thanks,' she said cautiously. She wore a new aubergine colored dress that had cost pretty much what her entire wardrobe had in her Indore days. A bunch of antique silver bracelets jangled on one arm, and she had taken a fair bit of effort over her make-up. Her reflection in the mirror told her she looked good—she just hadn't expected Sushil to notice. For the last few months he behaved as if she was about as alluring as a sack of potatoes.

'You were wearing the same colour on the first day of college.'

'Really?' Anjali asked. She had no recollection of it herself, though she vaguely remembered possessing a hideous jamuni coloured salwar kameez that she thought was the ultimate in chic attire.

'The colour suits you,' Sushil persisted, edging closer

to her. Anjali stared at him. Sushil's occasional lapses into nostalgia always made her want to giggle—on the other hand, the look in his eyes was making her pulse race. Three months of living chastely in the same house had been pretty hellish. If nostalgia did the trick for Sushil, she wasn't going to object.

There was a little noise at the door, and they swung around to see Daffy looking at them interestedly. 'Sorry, am I interrupting?' she asked. 'Only I'm terribly hungry, and I thought I'd help hurry up dinner a bit.'

Anjali gave her an amused look. It would never even occur to Daffy to be embarassed about walking in on people during a tender moment. Luckily Sushil seemed to find her equally amusing.

'What's the latest gossip, Daffy?' he asked. 'Has Zina found herself a new boyfriend yet?'

'No, she hasn't,' Daffy said, her forehead creasing into a worried frown. 'That's unusual isn't it? Unless there's someone she's not talking about.'

'That Shiven guy again?' Anjali asked. 'That would be pretty disastrous.'

'No, not him,' Daffy said. 'Actually, if you ask me, I think she's still in love with the kid she was dating.'

Anjali's brows flew up. 'Ishaan?' she asked. 'Here, Sushil, you can carry this outside.' She gave Sushil a large casserole of dal, and turned back to Daffy.

'Was she serious about Ishaan?' she asked. 'I thought it was just the novelty factor.' To Anjali, Ishaan seemed only slightly older than Gayatri. He was quite amazingly good-looking of course, but then so were the kids in Johnson's baby shampoo ads. She made a mental note to sound Dr Suhasini on the subject.

'You were both brilliant,' Rehaan's wife said warmly as the title credits rolled.

'Ah, but I was more brilliant,' Rehaan said. 'Bet there are women across the country calling the TV station right now, begging for my number.'

'What a pity they can't see you now,' Zina said sorrowfully. 'You look hotter than you ever have before.' In honour of the launch of the show, she had used face paints to give Rehaan a clown makeover; he was also wearing a multicoloured wig and a luridly checked shirt.

'Ah, I love you anyway, jaan,' Rehaan's wife said, and gave him a smacking kiss on his cheek as she handed him their brand-new daughter. 'Her diaper needs changing—can you go do it while I get dessert on the table?'

That was the kind of relationship she'd never have, Zina mused as she got into a cab after the party. Not that she wanted exactly what Rehaan and Shirin had—the thought of changing a diaper made her feel distinctly queasy. But being loved unconditionally when you'd just had a baby and were twelve kilos overweight had to count for something. Fretfully she glanced at her phone. It was late morning in Chicago, and Ishaan knew that her show was going on air today because he messaged her wishing good luck. She had assumed he'd call—he had been in touch on and off ever since he left, though in a 'just good friends' kind of way. Unconsciously, her hands clenched into fists. She *wanted* Ishaan. She thought about him all the time till he became a kind of obsession.

Ishaan didn't call, though dozens of her friends did. Even her normally clueless parents called, and more than a hundred people 'liked' the Facebook post where she announced the time of the show. Perhaps it was time to put up an official Facebook page—maybe even a website. The PR girl had suggested she get a little more active on social media; there were courses she could do, or the PR girl could help her. Zina gave an exasperated little sigh. There was no point pretending to herself. A year ago, all this would have mattered to the exclusion of everything else—right now, all she could think about was Ishaan.

She went to bed immediately after she got to her room, but it took a long while for her to get to sleep. When she finally did doze off, she dreamt of going onto set, and realising no one else was there, then putting on the TV and seeing Rehaan do the show with Daffy, giving Anjali a make-over. Then the dream shifted, and she was walking down a dark street, following a man. However fast she walked, he stayed several paces ahead of her, not turning even when she called out.

It was morning when she woke up, feeling hardly rested. Actually strike that, she felt as if she had run a marathon and *then* spent the night digging ditches. Groaning, she rubbed her eyes a few times before opening them. 'Eeks,' she said as her gaze fell on Daffy who was perched on a writing desk and looking at her owlishly. She was dressed in a neon pink, extremely tight tracksuit, and her hair was standing up on end like the guy's in the CentreShock ad. To add to the generally bizarre effect, she also had on some kind of a translucent face-mask that gave her skin a shiny, greenish tinge.

'Good morning,' Daffy said solemnly.

Zina struggled to a sitting position. 'You could give me a heart attack, creeping up on me like that,' she complained. 'Why've you got pond scum on your face?'

'It's a new face pack Anjali recommended,' Daffy said, sounding offended. 'And I came here to call you because your boyfriend's waiting downstairs, and he can't get through to you on your phone. You've let it drain out of charge as usual I expect.'

'Ishaan...?' Zina wondered if she was still asleep and dreaming. 'Are you sure?'

'Yes, I saw him myself.' Daffy slid off the desk. 'And you should wash your face before rushing down to see him. You look a bit like a racoon.'

Hmm, Daffy was right, Zina thought peering at herself in a mirror. She had collapsed into bed the night before without bothering to remove her make-up, and her eye-shadow had smudged badly. Assuming it *was* Ishaan downstairs and Daffy wasn't hallucinating, she'd need to do some quick repairs.

Ishaan was amusing himself by reading the notices in the visitor's room. Zina stood at the door for a minute, gazing at him hungrily. He no longer looked thin and tired the way he had for months after the surgery—his shoulders had filled out, and his body had regained its athletic grace. And his profile was as perfect as ever, and his mouth as tempting. It took a fair degree of self-control not to run across the room and throw herself into his arms.

He turned at that moment, and gave her a slow smile. 'I loved the show,' he said. 'And you looked gorgeous.'

'I thought you were in Chicago,' she said stupidly, feeling too confused to even try going closer to him.

'I came back a couple of days ago,' he said. 'Are you free right now? Can I take you out for lunch?'

'It's eleven o'clock,' Zina said. 'I haven't even had breakfast yet.'

'Breakfast followed by lunch then,' he said. 'Come over to my place.'

Zina instinctively glanced down at her clothes. She had pulled on a pair of shorts and a faded T-shirt to come downstairs, and there was no way she could land up in Dr Suhasini's immaculate home looking like a rag-picker's assistant.

'No one's at home,' Ishaan informed her kindly. 'Mom's in the US for a conference, and Alisha's at a friend's birthday party.'

'I still need to change,' Zina said. 'Why don't you go over to the coffee shop across the road, and I'll be there in ten minutes.'

Feeling a lot more human once she had showered and changed into clean jeans and a loose chiffon top, Zina went to find Ishaan. He had nabbed a corner table at the coffee shop and was interestedly leafing through a fashion magazine that a previous customer had left behind.

'I had a bit of an epiphany last week,' he said as he pushed a cup of her favourite coffee across. 'I told you before I left, long-distance relationships aren't really my thing.' 'So you found yourself a girl in Chicago?' Zina asked, all hope that he had changed his mind about long-distance relationships evaporating. Perhaps it would hurt less if she said it, and he only had to nod in agreement. To her intense annoyance, he said nothing at all, just picked up his coffee and took a sip.

'My mom's thinking of retiring, did I tell you that?' he asked after a while. Zina shook her head. The thought of Dr Suhasini retiring was unsettling—she was one of those people whose profession was so ingrained in their personalities that you didn't think of them having a life outside work.

'Well, she is,' Ishaan said. 'She wants to spend time with Alisha before the kid grows up and leaves home.'

'I suppose that makes sense,' Zina said, not being able to think of anything more insightful. 'You were saying something about long-distance...umm...not being really your thing...'

'Yeah,' Ishaan said. 'On second thoughts, this isn't the best place for a conversation. If you're done with your coffee, should we go to my place? I can't talk with people staring at us.'

It was probably the first time in his life that Ishaan was finding it difficult to talk, but instead of pulling his leg about it, Zina gulped the rest of the coffee down in such a hurry that she scalded her throat.

The drive to Ishaan's flat normally took fifteen minutes—today, of course there were two wedding processions and one broken-down truck on the road, and it took almost an hour.

'D'you like studying in the US?' Zina asked after a bit, when it became clear that Ishaan was as uncomfortable talking about relationships in cars as he was in coffee shops.

'It's brilliant,' Ishaan said. 'Though sometimes I wish I'd stuck with the original plan of doing a gap year. Most of the guys in my year did that, and I'm tired of hearing their stories.'

'Right,' Zina said, trying to look intelligent. She had heard about gap years before, but where?

'Take a year off from studies,' Ishaan supplied. 'Travel, learn new languages, start a rock band—that kind of stuff. It's all about self-discovery.'

It sounded more like complete self-indulgence to Zina. 'And who pays for the gap year?' she asked.

'In the US and Europe? You work through school and college and save up, and then you use your savings during the gap year. And you work part-time in a bar or a restaurant in whichever country you travel to. In India, well, it's still sort of a rich kid thing. I was planning to use some of the money my Dad left me.'

'I remember!' Zina said suddenly. 'They asked Anjali a question about letting Gayatri take a gap year in the Wellington interview. She thought it was a completely dumb idea, letting a kid take off for a year like that.'

'I wonder if she said that in the interview,' Ishaan said, laughing. 'Quite a few kids from my batch took a gap year immediately after school, and there was a lot of discussion around it.'

'Oh yes, you went to Wellington too,' Zina said. There was a certain level of comfort in talking about inane stuff. Soon she'd be asking him which brand of toothpaste he used. Except she already knew—Colgate Total, and he always left the cap off. The toothpaste thing brought back a host of memories, and she firmly put a lid on them. There would be time enough to get sentimental about his little quirks once he told her what he was up to.

The flat was exactly the same as Zina remembered it, except for Ishaan's room. The colour scheme and the furniture were the same, but the tennis rackets and the guitar and the untidy heaps of books were gone.

'Right, all clear,' Ishaan said, coming back into the room and shutting the door behind him with a decisive click. 'When I was sixteen I smuggled a girl into my room when I thought the flat was empty. Turns out my mother had come back early from work—it was pretty embarassing.'

'I bet,' Zina said, trembling with a mixture of anticipation and lust as he reached out for her. The kiss was explosive, and she had trouble staying upright when he finally let her go. Luckily she didn't have to try for long. In the next second, Ishaan was scooping her into his arms to deposit her on the bed. He stood for a second, looking down at her, his dark eyes dancing as she tried to pull him down on top of her.

'I assume you're okay with postponing our discussion for a bit,' he said as she started tugging at his shirt. 'Hmm,' Zina said, as she finally got the shirt off him so that her hands could roam freely over his chest. 'Yes, I think talking can wait.'

Around an hour later, Ishaan propped himself up on an elbow and slowly traced a finger down one side of her cheek. 'Not bad, considering how out of practice I am,' he said. It had been wonderful, and he knew it, but still Zina gave him a look of simulated disbelief. 'Not a single gori agreed to sleep with you?' she asked in horrified tones. 'Ishaan, you must be losing your touch. No wonder you came rushing across to meet me.'

His face sobered. 'That wasn't the reason,' he said, then corrected himself. 'At least it wasn't the only reason.' He cupped her face in his hands. 'Zina...stop me if you don't want to hear this, but I think I'm in love with you.' Misinterpreting her stunned expression, he went on hurriedly, 'I totally understand if you don't feel the same way. I've just not been able to stop thinking about you, and well...I wanted you to know. Just in case I still had a chance.'

'You utter idiot,' Zina said despairingly. 'I've been in love with you since the day I met you.' Reaching out, she pulled him into her arms. 'I think this calls for a celebration, don't you?'

By the end of the day they'd got everything settled. Ishaan had another year and a half to go before he completed his course—after that he'd get a job, and Zina would join him. And they'd visit each other in between, so it wouldn't be too bad.

'And no nonsense about gap years,' Zina told him severely. 'I can't believe you were seriously considering it.'

Ishaan gave her a wry look. 'Tells you how desperate I was,' he said. 'I thought I'd bribe you with a year of travelling around Europe on my Dad's money.'

'Running away while your mom chased us with an axe, more likely,' Zina retorted.

'Why did you say you didn't believe in long-term relationships?' she asked after a while.

'I genuinely thought you'd forget about me as soon as I was out of sight,' he said. 'And I'm a bit touchy like that, I didn't want to be dumped the second you met a more interesting guy.'

Dr Suhasini gave them both a resigned look when they told her. 'I had a feeling this might happen,' she said. 'I can't pretend I'm thrilled—I'd have liked Ishaan to concentrate on his studies instead of dreaming about getting married.'

'Oh, Zina'll make me concentrate all right,' Ishaan said cheerfully. 'If I don't, she'll run away with someone who has better prospects.'

'Ignore him, he just likes to wind people up,' Dr Suhasini said, noticing the stricken look on Zina's face. 'What about your TV career, Zina? It'll be tough to keep that going in a new country.'

'It's not as much fun as I thought it would be,' Zina said, making a face. 'Crazy hours, and people bitching about you all the time. I'll do the second run of the show with Rehaan, and then I'll go back to hairdressing. Maybe I could open a salon of my own some day.'

'A whole chain of them,' Ishaan said. He was bubbling over with happiness, and looking even more boyish than ever. 'You'll be the hairdresser to the stars, and I'll charge people tons of money for telling them how to run their companies.'

'And your children will turn into little baseball-playing Americans,' Dr Suhasini said.

'Ugh, children I hadn't even thought of that,' Zina said involuntarily. Though she had seen Ishaan's incredibly cute baby pictures—she wouldn't mind having just one son who looked just like him.

'We'll think about that later,' Ishaan said firmly. 'For the next ten years, I'll be too young to be a Dad.'

'Zina's back with Ishaan,' Daffy told Anjali excitedly.
'How nice,' Anjali said. 'I hope this time none of her ex-boyfriends lands up and tries to murder him.'

'You're growing terribly cynical, do you know that?' Daffy demanded. 'It's very odd, you weren't like this earlier.'

Daffy was right, she hadn't been like this earlier, Anjali thought as she put the phone down. It was the whole thing between her and Sushil. They were still being perfectly polite to each other, but after telling her she looked good on the day Zina's show went live, Sushil had gone right back to being remote and unavailable. A lot of it was her own fault—infuriated with Sushil, she had rebuffed him the first few times he had tentatively tried to make amends, and he stopped pretty soon. The problem was all the history between them. Having separated once, they were now dangerously close to splitting up again.

If the fight with Sushil had happened a little earlier when Gayatri had run away, Anjali would probably have just packed up and gone back to Indore. A large reason for moving to Mumbai was because she thought it was the best thing for Gayatri, and if Gayatri was unhappy, the move no longer made sense. But now, Gayatri *did* seem happy, and things with Sushil were definitely not bad enough for her to want to go back to Indore.

Her phone rang, and she stiffened as she looked at the display. She and Deven Khatri had reached an unspoken understanding not to stay in touch once she was back with Sushil. Or at least that was what she thought.

Gingerly she picked up the phone. 'Hello,' she said.

'Hi,' Deven said, sounding as awkward as she felt. 'I hope I'm not calling at a bad time. I just happened to be in Mumbai, so I thought I'd give you a ring.'

Not a diamond one I hope, Anjali almost said, but pulled herself back in time. Deven didn't appreciate facetiousness—Sushil on the other hand loved puns and PJs. No wonder she was back with Sushil. Deven hadn't stood a chance once Sushil was back.

'How's everything?' he was asking sombrely. 'I heard about Gayatri coming back to Indore alone, is everything okay?'

'Everything's fine,' she said. 'Just about perfect, in fact. Which part of Mumbai are you in, Deven?'

'I'm staying with a friend in Vasai,' he said. Anjali wrinkled her nose. Vasai, Vasai, where had she heard the name of that place before? She had a vague impression of it being very far, almost outside the city.

'But I'm in town tomorrow,' he said. 'And as it was your birthday, I thought I'd drop by and wish you.'

'Yes, of course,' Anjali said graciously. Her birthday had luckily fallen on a Saturday. Unluckily, however, her family showed no signs of remembering it, and in the current circumstances, she could hardly remind Sushil.

'So I'll drop by at around six in the evening then,' Deven said eagerly.

Sushil put the phone down with a sigh of relief. Without Devika, he'd be completely lost trying to organise a surprise birthday party. Even now, he felt like he was way out of his depth, but she had broken the whole thing down into simple, easily manageable tasks. Call the caterers. Order a cake. Invite Anjali's friends. Swear them all to secrecy. Figure out a way of getting Anjali out of the house in the evening so that everyone could sneak in.

Surreptitiously, he crossed his fingers behind his back. Apologising didn't come naturally to him, and he was hoping that a surprise birthday party for Anjali would indicate he was sorry, and also be a gesture that was grand enough to bring her around. He had got her a gift of course, and wished her in the morning, but he saved the grand surprise for the evening.

It was seven in the morning when Anjali woke the next morning. Gayatri was standing next to her with an expectant look on her face. 'Happy birthday,' she said abruptly as soon as Anjali's eyes fluttered open. 'Here's your gift! Hope you like it.' The gift was a handmade papier-mâché bowl that had been lovingly painted with an intricate design of vines and flowers. 'It's to hold your hair-clips and stuff,' Gayatri said, and Anjali got up and gave her a hug. They'd always done handmade gifts for each other in Indore—of course they'd splurged on store-bought gifts as well, but the main gift was always something that they'd slaved over for days before the birthday.

'Happy birthday,' Sushil said awkwardly, handing her a neatly-wrapped present, very evidently store-bought and store-wrapped. 'Thanks,' Anjali said, hating how formal she sounded. She opened the box carefully to find a delicate gold bracelet inside, studded with small diamonds that glittered and sparkled in the sunlight that was peeking through the curtains. 'It's pretty,' she said, meaning it, but he clearly thought she was being polite, because his expression closed up. 'It's nothing much, I wasn't sure what to get,' he said, and backed out of the room.

'Cheer up, at least he didn't give you a washing machine,' Devika said when Anjali told her. Devika had helped pick the bracelet up—Sushil's taste veered towards being over-the-top. She also had a fair idea of how things were between Anjali and Sushil, but like Sushil, she was hoping that the air would get cleared up after the party.

'But he thought I hated it,' Anjali wailed. 'So I thought I'd tell you because I bet you chose it for him. Left to himself he'd have gone and bought something utterly gross.'

'I did choose it, and that's exactly why he knows you don't hate it,' Devika said. 'Now, how about I take you out for a little treat at around six? You'll be back in time to go out for dinner with Sushil and Gayatri.' This was the excuse with which they'd planned to get Anjali out of the house while Sushil set up everything for the party.

'Can't,' Anjali said succinctly. 'I've got an old friend coming over at six.'

Devika thought Sushil would have a heart attack. 'What old friend?' he demanded.

'She's not told me anything about this. Some woman from Indore,' Devika said. Anjali hadn't specified the gender of the friend, and Devika had assumed it was a woman. 'Don't worry about it, we'll just move everything to seven. I guarantee I'll have her out of the house by then.'

While Anjali agreed quite readily to meet Devika at six-forty five, when it was actually time, her phone kept ringing, and she didn't pick up.

The reason was five feet eleven inches tall, and was sitting in her living room making an impassioned plea for her to reconsider his proposal. 'I wouldn't have said a word if you were happy with him, but you're not,' Deven said. 'I know I can't give you as much as he can,' he made a sweeping gesture that encompassed the luxurious flat they were sitting in, 'But I'll make sure that you're happy, and so is Gayatri.'

'I'm perfectly happy,' Anjali said, hoping her nose wouldn't grow longer with the lie. 'And so is Gayatri.' The doorbell rang, and she greeted the sound with relief. The relief was replaced with sudden dismay however, as she opened the door and found Anil Nair standing outside. He was carrying a massive bouquet of orchids, and a perfectly gift-wrapped parcel that looked as if it contained books.

Anil still didn't know that he had been the unwitting cause of so much friction between Sushil and Anjali. Anjali had been too embarrassed to tell him, and Sushil didn't see the need.

'Happy birthday,' Anil said, smiling at her. 'I'm sorry, is this a bad time? I did try calling—couldn't get through, so I thought I'd drop these off.'

It would have been completely churlish not to have invited him in, so Anjali stepped back and held the door open as she thanked him prettily for the flowers and the gift. Deven was anything but pleased though, and he fell into a morose silence after Anjali introduced the two of them.

The doorbell rang for a third time, and Anjali went to open the door, hoping it wasn't yet another embarrassing visitor. Thankfully it was Devika this time, understandably annoyed about her calls not being answered. 'Let's go now,' she said, tugging at Anjali's arm. She promised Sushil she'd have Anjali out of the flat in ten minutes, but the way things were going, it looked like it would take an hour.

She texted Sushil: She's got visitors. We'll need to wait till they leave.

He texted back: Who?

Guy called Deven Khatri, and one of her students, Anil Nair.

If Devika had known the effect her SMS would have, she'd have thought a dozen times before sending it. Probably she'd have told Anjali about the party, and bundled the two men out of the door, trusting Anjali's acting skills as far as the 'surprise' element of the party went.

Sushil let himself into the flat ten minutes later. He had had some time to think, and he figured that making a fuss wouldn't help. Appearances notwithstanding, it wasn't like Anjali was holding an orgy in the flat. Actually, if only one man had been there, Sushil would have been suspicious. With both of them being there at the same time, the maximum Anjali could do was hold a swayamvara, albeit one in which the princess was already married with a twelve-year-old daughter. And if that was what she was doing, he definitely needed to be there.

Anjali's face, as he came into the room, held no trace of apprehension or guilt. If anything, she looked positively relieved. Must be the Deven guy, Sushil thought as he began to see the funny side of things. 'You're home early,' she said, and he nodded, wondering how to handle the situation. Deven was looking obviously uncomfortable—Anil's expression was as inscrutable as ever, but Sushil got the impression that he wasn't pleased to see him either.

'Anjali, should we...' he began to say, but his words were drowned out by around forty people piling into the room and yelling 'Surprise!' all at once.

Anjali looked totally flummoxed. Daffy and Erik were there, so was Kavita, and Devika of course was already in the flat. Zina was standing to one side, with Ishaan next to her, and Lydia was smiling and blowing kisses at everyone in sight.

The doorbell rang again, as the caterer and cake arrived together, both evidently tired of waiting.

'I think I should go,' Anil murmured, standing up, but Sushil put a jovial arm around his and Deven's shoulders. 'Stay for a bit,' he said.

In the confusion, Sushil's eyes sought Anjali's. She was watching him with an odd, arrested look on her face, as if the last bit of a jigsaw puzzle had finally fallen into place.

Not wanting any more confusion, Sushil rapped on the dining table for silence. As everyone turned to look at him, he said, 'As the husband of the birthday girl, I'd like to make a very short speech. Anjali and I lived apart from each other because I was working in Saudi Arabia and it's not very comfortable for women there. We moved to Mumbai a little less than a year ago, and while nothing's perfect, I do believe that we've now come as close to perfection as possible.' He paused to give Deven Khatri a quelling look before he went on. 'I'd like to raise a toast to my beautiful and talented wife, whom I love even more today than when we were first dating in college.'

Anjali's eyes brimmed over, and she came across the room to throw herself into Sushil's arms. 'I love you too,' she mumbled into his chest. Then she lifted her head and looked up at him, her eyes laughing into his. 'Sushil, for the first time since we came to Mumbai, I can look around and say that this feels like home.'

Sushil looked around as well, and he nodded slowly. 'Yes, it does,' he said. 'And it'll be even better once we get this lot fed and out of here!'

Made in the USA
Monee, IL
03 May 2026